KNIGHT RESCUE

JP WILDER

EDGE WEAVER LLC

Knight Rescue

Edge Weaver Realms is an imprint of Edge Weaver LLC

Book Two of the Crusader Series

Book Design: Marie Pitrat

Kindle ISBN: 978-1-964406-16-9

Paperback ISBN: 978-1-964406-80-0

Published in the United States of America

Edge Weaver LLC
19360 Rinaldi #681
Porter Ranch, CA 91326-1607

CONTENTS

CHAPTER 1
THE STONE

"Without more evidence than your hunch, I cannot and will not challenge the bishop," knight Commander Gavreaux announced to me as he stared back, matching me sneer for sneer. He was tall and broad-shouldered, and his gait and movements were fluid. He was a man built for combat. A single scar crossed his face, and his short beard seemed to have turned grayer in the months since he and a group of his knights had saved me from certain death on the spearheads of Golish cavalry.

That was a bittersweet day for me. Indeed, the Commander had saved me, but my charge, Edweene, had gone down beneath sword and spear. But somehow, she'd survived. I shook the dark thoughts away. As bitter as it was, it had solidified my debt to Gavreaux and enhanced his position in my eyes—and the position of the Knights of the Holy Passage. Since then, I'd returned to the Holy Land with my contingent of Crusaders, now encamped outside Clurak with my captain, Ser Wilhem, awaiting my return. I figured—given my objectives—it would be a long wait for the young knight.

Gavreaux stood behind a tall, finely carved dark-wood chair that was adorned with worn leather cushions on the seat and back. Ten paces behind him, a wide, iron-bound door provided entry and egress for him, different from those of us who were invited here. A broad table of the same hardwood as the chairs stood between us. Upon it, a single tankard of dark liquid sat near his seat, untouched.

I stood next to a matching chair on my side of the table, my hand on its back. If it had been dark, the cold room would have been lit with two large candlesticks at either end of the table—one to my right and one to my left. As it was, the waning light of day did a fine job keeping the room in gray haze and shadow.

Gavreaux frowned at me.

A Thayne, sworn to the king of Bannon, who had answered the call of the Archbishop and sallied on the Crusade, should not be questioning the motives of the Bishop of Tears or his loyalties to the king of Clurak. But there I was, looking Gavreaux in the eye, telling him that the Archbishop's representative in the Holy Land, His Excellency Bishop Tooleb of Tears, was a traitor to the Crusade.

The irony was obvious to me—a killer accusing another of murder, or at least the attempting of it.

"Even entertaining this mad line of discussion could have me put to the sword, or worse." Gavreaux turned away from me and peered out of his austere war room over the towering walls of the ancient fortress, The Stone.

The Stone had stood for a thousand years. Before the Coming of The God, when Clurak and all the Northern Kingdoms were part of the Empire of Travanah, our forebears built the Stone, which has stood for a thousand years. But those days had perished long ago, along with the worship of the Old Gods in the Eastern and Northern Kingdoms. The fort had changed hands more times since then, than one could count. But you could still see the reflection of past occupiers, both Imperial and Gol.

Once vital to defending against invasion by Western raiders a thousand years ago, the Stone's location had become marginalized in the conflicts surrounding the Holy Land. In each of the Crusades, Clurak or more strategic strongholds were under threat by Golish armies, and the Stone served as a landing point and logistics center for forays into the land. It was too far off the main track to become strategic beyond that purpose. Its most important function for the last two hundred years had been to house the headquarters for the largest Chivalric Order in the Holy Land: The Knights of the Holy Passage. It also marked the westernmost area of the Order's influence.

Passage Knights did not foray west of the Stone, even in the escort of pilgrims. Those were the lands patrolled by the Knights of Tears—the Holy Order of knights sworn to protect the Holy City and the Temple of Tears. The Knights of Passage had no desire to tangle with the Tears and the series of lunatics that had stood atop that Order for the better part of a century. And I knew it—it was knowledge common to all but the most ignorant in the Holy Land. That was one reason I was here, meeting with Lord Gavreaux, and not meeting with knight Commander Transom of the Tears. He was a dogmatic fiend, and my conversation with Gavreaux would have resulted in my flaying on The Star of The God if I had broached it with Transom. The other reason was straightforward: I trusted this particular zealot. He'd saved my life once, only months before, despite his predilections otherwise. I was convinced that he believed in the truth of my cause, even if he didn't agree with my methods.

"You have been spinning this tale, Ser, in the Capital beneath the king's own roof. Too many unfriendly ears have witnessed it. Your lack of discretion causes me much discomfort in even meeting with you. I fear the only reason that fat bishop hasn't had you flayed is your popularity among the people of the North—poor country knight, the Savior of Clurak—not once, but twice by The God, hang on to that, man. I'd hate to see you missing that hide of yours."

I winced. Truer words were probably never said. I was lucky to avoid death and punishment, as providential events saved me from being considered an enemy of the Church. And that meant that this conversation was going nowhere. I wanted to believe that Gavreaux was a fool or a coward, but I knew he was neither. Him not having me flayed or strung up in the keep's bailey told me he may even have had some of the same concerns, but he would not move on the bishop without evidence, whether or not he was brave, or intelligent. Crossing the bishop meant crossing the archbishop, which meant crossing The God. And a holy warrior such as Gavreaux would be hard-pressed to make that leap. My time here was wasted, a fool's notion—as I had thought it might be when I saddled my horse in Clurak weeks ago and made the trek.

Gavreaux turned away from me once more, his gaze distant, as if wrestling with some inner turmoil. The silence stretched between us, heavy with unspoken words and conflicting loyalties. Finally, he seemed to decide, his shoulders squaring as he faced me again.

"Though I will not condemn the bishop, I have a proposition for you, my lord," he said, his eyes cast down, mannerisms almost submissive. "If you are willing," he whispered, it seemed to me, apologetically. It was strange for a man such as him to emit such mannerisms, and it was a moment filled with discomfort for me. He continued staring at the ground.

"Yes, my lord," I said, trying to keep my interest at bay.

He coughed, seemed to find himself, and raised his eyes to me. He straightened his back, stood tall, and said, "It is a proposition I am not proud of, but one that I think you will excel at."

My interest was more than a little piqued. What could make this man want to contract with someone of my repute—a dishonorable assassin, to use Gavreaux's own words from months before—for his purposes? It was one thing for me to reach out to him for help on a matter that carried the gravity of a bishop's betrayal. But for him to reach out to me? It was not even in the realm of honor.

"A proposition?" I asked.

He cleared his throat loudly, covering it with a gloved fist. "Yes," he started. "A column of Lord Richeau's knights forayed beyond the Knuckles and surprised a formation of Golish infantry. Not knowing where they were—meaning, as you know, that they no longer stood in the protectorate of the Holy Land—Richeau's expedition fell upon the heathens, cutting them down."

I gaped at him. The Knuckles were a series of fortifications that had marked the end of The Crusader state and the Gol's lands. Passing them in force brought the risk of war between Gol and the Crusaders. "The fools," said I. "They'll ignite the war with such acts of stupidity."

The Earl Richeau was the Lord of An Andor, a large holding midway between The Stone and An Kolnaak. It was an important land in so much as it straddled the Pilgrim's Approach and was a major thoroughfare for pilgrimages, merchants, and military trains. The Earl was a powerful noble—the brother of Earl Teneaux of Ri Lisana. He obtained the holding for so-called heroic deeds during the Second Crusade, and he was a favorite at the court of Lethan, King of Clurak, the Holy Defender. I did not know the man well—one could say not at all—but he had a reputation for mad cavalry charges and foolhardy gambles. He was not a man whose banner I would gladly follow.

Gavreaux's eyes flashed at me.

Something I said? I wondered.

"Precisely what the king said when he was asked to pay ransom," said he.

"Ransom?" I asked.

"Yes," he said. "Ransom."

"I understood the knights were victorious by your statement, Ser," I said.

"They were," he looked away. "Initially," he added.

"Initially," I repeated his last word as if the man were stupid or I was deaf. "What fool's plan did they pursue after this massacre?" I asked.

He glared at me then, clearly angry, said, "Careful your tongue, Ser. These were knights and men-at-arms sworn to the king and The God."

I don't know why I should be surprised at the stupidity of our race of men. We continue to make the same errors and then make excuses or apologies for our actions as if tradition trumps wisdom. This action could have reignited the war. Still, I should have known better than to insult knights and Lords loyal to The God. Civilization needs its ordering, I suppose. "I apologize, Ser," I said. "Sometimes my mouth outruns my mind."

"Ahh . . ." he started and waved his hand, as if to say, *nevermind*. And then he spoke again, "You are right. It was a foolish endeavor that I would scold them for if they now stood before me."

I bowed my head and thanked him for his grace, inwardly mocking the madness of our tradition. Men were dead or captured, and we worried about the proper respect paid their titles and not the stupidity of their mad foray into the land of the Gols. "You had said, my lord, that they 'were knights and men-at-arms sworn to the king and The God'," I emphasized the word *were* and let it hang for the smallest moment.

The Lord Commander looked at me as if I was his enemy. His eyes narrowed, and I thought he might strike me. He sighed then and seemed to soften, shoulders drooping. "Yes. Yes, I did."

"Does this imply their demise?" I asked at last.

"Their sortie did not end there," he said. He sat down in his tall chair. He motioned me down. I obliged, settling into the hard leather seat. He reached up and grabbed the tankard that had been growing warm there and slurped deeply the contents. "Apparently, their victory fueled their confidence, and they sallied westward, following the Gol infantry's track. But there must have been Golish scouts on the heights, for when the knights entered the hilly area some distance south and west of their last massacre, a formation of Tartans—horse and foot, both, set upon them."

I inhaled deeply. "Tartans—it is a lucky thing that any are alive. They rarely take prisoners."

Unless they consider the prisoner to be important. They knew by his banner that this man was
significant to the king—at least to his men."

"Not important enough, I wager," I said, wishing I had a tankard of ale to wet my mouth. I was
beginning to see the way of things, to understand
Gavreaux's purpose.

"The king has chosen not to pay the ransom, as
has the bishop. I would like this knight back. He
is important to me."

"Why would the king not pay the ransom? Why
would you not pay this ransom? Surely you have
the means."

"The foray was unsanctioned by the king—or
the Temple for that matter. His Grace is making
a point—an example of this knight to those lords
on the Crusade who may think to take matters
into their own hands. The knight, his Grace says,
must face his mortality for denying the providence of The God."

"And what would you have me do?" I asked,
already figuring out the right answer. War and
loss do things to people. They make them go
down roads they'd never consider in normal cir-

cumstances. I saw in this man's eyes that he was about to cross a threshold here, to go somewhere he didn't want to go.

"I would have you rescue this knight," he said. His eyes caught mine in a stare so intense that I could not draw my head away. His gaze was hard, challenging, pleading.

I sat forward, elbows on the table, hands tented under my chin. "And you? Why don't you take your knights to free him or pay the ransom yourself?"

"Ser, they have forbidden me," he said, reaching into his surcoat and pulling out a folded piece of parchment affixed with a broken seal. He tossed it across the table toward me and took another swig of his drink

I reached over and took the parchment. The king's seal, broken apart, was affixed to it. I unfolded it carefully and read the words there:

Lord Commander Gavreaux,

I am sad to hear of this knight's plight. I am sure that you understand why I cannot pay the ransom demanded to the heathen dogs that took him. I also am sure that you understand why I require that you take no action to free him, either by force or financial means. We must establish discipline among the Holy and strive to maintain our control over the host. Doing otherwise would jeopardize our standing among the Crusaders and encourage a breakdown in order.

By Royal Decree—

Lethan, Defender of the Holy Land and king of Clurak.

I closed the letter and slid it back across to him. I understood why there would be no ransom. The king must make a point, or others might follow this man's poor example. He could not have his knights and men-at-arms taking missions unto themselves. Tempers on both sides of the Knuckles were already out of hand. Two large, restless armies had been formed with nothing to do but pillage and plunder their cities. Still, abandoning his man seemed un-kingly, even denying others the right to pay the ransom. How did that inspire confidence in those who followed him? Ruling with such tactics only worked if the king showed his armies his loyalty in other, greater ways. I doubted that King Lethan showed loyalty to his men at all. Despite all that being true to me, I was still surprised that the Lord Commander would condescend to subterfuge to release this captured knight, and I voiced my surprise. "Last time we spoke, you did not approve of my methods, Ser Gavreaux. A man with your strict adherence to your betters should not be considering such actions as this," I said.

"My sister, you see . . ." he said as if ignoring my point ". . . is Monae Baudin, Earless of An Andor. This young knight is Ser Prenot, her son. She would very much like her son returned to her."

A moment of clarity, it was, and suddenly it all made sense to me.

"For the price of his rescue," he began again, "I will assist you in this endeavor of yours. I cannot directly confront the bishop or his man, Transom. But I can make available to you my network, find your information and perhaps put some bug in the king's ear. For, if war starts, his throne bears the most risk. And the knight Commander of Tears bears the greatest probability of reward, standing as he does, ready to receive the crown if Lethan falls. The camp, I am told is merely two days into the Devil's Forest from the closest knuckle."

I thought for a moment. The mission was intriguing, but it could delay my sworn vengeance by weeks or months or more. Though the young knight surely needed saving, it would not be me who would do it. I said, "I am sorry, my lord. I feel for this young knight, your nephew, but I must continue my mission. It is a matter of honor," I said. I could not meet his eyes. I had likely just doomed his nephew to death. I thought he would understand the reason, but my act seemed to me to sound hollow and selfish, even if I had convinced myself otherwise.

He sighed. It was heavy with burden and resignation. A long, dark moment passed. "Very well," he said. "War is what it always has been. Our loved ones perish. And we carry on. It is the way of things. The boy shall pay for his error."

I looked down at the table, the gritty sorrow in his eyes too much for me to bear.

Gavreaux stood again and extended his hand across the table to me. I took it. His grip was steel.

It said *no hard feelings*. I almost choked with guilt. "I am disappointed that we could not reach an agreement," he said. "Despite that, I cannot in good conscience withhold my help from you if I have similar concerns regarding our Holy Bishop. So, I will see what help I can provide for you on this bishop endeavor, but it must remain hidden. Expect no miracles. You shall hear from my man soon." He pushed back his chair, turned his back, and strode for the back entry.

"Yes, my lord," I struggled to say to his rapidly retreating back. I stood and stumbled backward, then turned for the door. I remember thinking that I had just witnessed one.

CHAPTER 2
EDWEENE

I walked the distance to the bailey gate, deep in thought, my boots crunching over the gravelly courtyard. The evening was coming. The sun, brilliant in the east just moments before, was dropping behind the Sea of Sorrows, turning the sky orange, and the waters blood red. Behind the tall stone walls of the keep, the shadows were long on the ground and black as night around sharp corners. A feeling of melancholy—of judgment fell over me.

I could not have asked for more than I got. But leaving the Knight Commander that way tugged at my conscience. Tartans captured his nephew in an unsanctioned mission. That did not bode well for Ser Prenot. What would I do if this were my nephew under some enemy's boot? I did not like the answer that kept coming to my mind.

Of course, the Knight Commander could have invoked my debt to him, but he is not a man who would do so. Did I have a responsibility to repay my debt this way if he did not ask me for it? Did my vengeance and mission not carry more weight than this man's foolhardy nephew? I decided it was so, but a feeling of guilt nagged at my heart.

I told myself that there was no way that I could undertake this mission if I were to find my vengeance in a suitable time frame—that the bishop's betrayal held larger implications for the Holy Land. The knight had made a mistake, and now he would pay. Such was the way of things here in the Holy Land. Besides, I had sworn vengeance on those who had betrayed the king's mission in my last duty—those who had tried to ambush and murder me. I was determined to follow through on my sworn duty, even if that duty was to my own sense of rage and vengeance.

The hard part in all of this—the true immediate challenge—was proving that my hunch was right—that it was the bishop who had tried to kill me, who wanted my last mission to fail, and the war to go on. If indeed it was, then I had to find a way to kill him or uncover his betrayal to the king in such a way that everyone accepted it as The God's truth. How was I to do such a thing? The bishop was beyond censure—an agent of The God himself.

"This mission was no mistake. Prenot made no error," a voice slid out of the shadows.

I jerked to a stop in surprise. I drew my knife from my waist and faced the sound. The night was cool, the shadows in that direction dark as pitch behind a corner of the bailey's stable. The roof of the stable was designed as a makeshift walkway that served as a battlement atop the Stone's keep, and embrasures were constructed atop the wall, throwing dark shadows down in a strange alternating pattern of black and gray. The man could be in any one of these shadows.

To my left—in the opposite direction—the bailey opened up broadly into a wide, empty courtyard of sorts. The gate was ahead—a hundred paces—a bloody orange opening into the evening. A shiver ran down my spine. I looked quickly about for the raven and saw nothing. I would face this alone.

"You will not need your dagger, Ser," The invisible man said in a voice tinged with an accent from Leonay. "Our missions are intertwined."

"Show yourself," I said, my thumb playing over the intricately laid family crest on the crosspiece of my long knife. It was a habit of mine, which I knew I should break. "I do not discuss such things with shadowy figures in doorways. And how would you know of my mission?" Only minutes had passed, so I wondered if Gavreaux had contacted his agents this quickly. I thought not, but I asked anyway. "Are you Gavreaux's man?" I did not put my knife away.

"No. I am not his man," he answered quickly—perhaps too quickly for my liking. "The keep is not as secure as you might think. If one was familiar with its construction, he might find a way to listen to secret discussions between plotting Lords."

A lump worked its way into my throat. Was this man an agent of the bishop or, perhaps the king—maybe some other malevolent party? "I have no idea of what you a speaking, Ser," I said, as I rotated my body in a half-circle, facing the shadowy area where this man was likely hidden. I held my knife in front of me. "Come out," I demanded again as if that demand would somehow compel him.

To my surprise, it did. A man stepped from the darkened corner of the barrack side. He was tall and girded in steel. The faint outline of a small five-pointed star—or was it two?—was stitched above an embroidered horse's head on the red surcoat that covered his cuirass. He wore his steel comfortably, and he carried a full-visored helmet under his right arm, as is proper among knights. On his hip, a glimmer of polished steel told of a long sword's pommel, barely visible in the shadows. The darkness obscured his face so that I could not place his visage.

His voice was that of a young man, though edgy and filled with bitterness. "As I was saying, Ser, our missions are intertwined." His left hand squeezed his sword belt's buckle.

"And what might our missions be?"

"The bishop and the rescue of Ser Gavreaux's kin."

I turned toward him, squaring up, my dagger before me, in case this was some elaborate trap to lure me close. But, he kept his right hand—his sword hand—occupied with his helm. There was little threat here, I figured. I did not lower my guard. I'd been fooled before. "And which mission is yours—and which is mine?" I asked, feeling him out for how much he might know of me.

"You seek vengeance on the bishop," he said. "For what, I surely don't know, nor do I care." He shifted, his steel-shod feet scraping across the gravelly earth. "I seek the knight. I would free him if I could. We could work together. I shall help you with your bishop. You shall assist me in freeing the young lord."

I was surprised, even at the small bit he knew, but would not let him know as much. "Wishing harm upon the bishop is a crime against The God," I said, "Worthy of breaking on the Star," I said. "And even if I were seeking such unholy reprisal, why would I put it on hold for this knight rescue?" I asked. "If indeed I was to seek violence—or justice—against his Holiness, should I not be on my way sooner than later, lest he send his men against me?" I paced toward him as I spoke. I wanted to get a better look at his face. But, the man stepped back, deeper into the shadows.

"I think, Ser," he responded, "You will find that rescuing Ser Prenot will further your ambitions and provide you much-needed intelligence with which to prosecute your undertaking."

The night lapsed to silence. His breathing was heavy in the silence of the night. My heartbeat throbbed in my chest. Was this some clue for me to follow up on? Or was this a trap, set by those who might be against me, to find me complicit in an unholy scheme? I decided it was not worth the risk. But, before I could respond, he said, "Think about it, Ser." He turned from me and strode into the darkness.

After he left, I continued to my room. I made no effort to follow him, as I was concerned about ambush, or seeming too interested. I thrust open the door to my chamber—a small apartment set aside near the barrack where the men-at-arms laid their heads when not drilling. It was likely the room for some low-level knight or Sergeant close by the barrack so that he might keep an eye on the footmen—one responsible for drilling them and keeping them sharp. It was, however, unoccupied for the time being, so the Lord Commander had found it useful to billet me there. It was no wonder why I was not allowed in the keep. I was not well-liked among those most loyal to the Temple—I was a disturber of the peace, as it were. It would not show well for one such as Ser Gavreaux to keep me that close and provide me with that level of hospitality.

Regardless of the reason, the small room was where I had stowed my gear. It had a rickety wooden bed, covered in heavy wool blankets and a small writing table with two tall candleholders atop it. A small chair was set beside the table. A tiny window was set in the wall, next to the door, opening into the courtyard. There was nothing else. It was small and scant. It was perfect. I needed nothing else. The candles were doused. The room was pitch.

I was tired and disturbed by the specter-like knight in the courtyard. I did not bother lighting the candles and immediately began to struggle out of my armor. Normally, a knight of my rank—a Thayne, as you may remember—would have the help of a handy squire to assist with such things. But, I had not brought a squire with me, even after my man, Ser Willem—the captain of the contingent of footmen and sworn knights that I had brought from Riverdale—had suggested I should. It was not befitting a Thayne such as me to be traveling the land without his assistant, he'd said to me. But, I had passed on the idea, leaving the man to help Willem with the regulation of my Thaynehold's contribution to the Crusade—ten knights and seventy-five footmen that carried my River and Lion on their shields. Truth be known, I had never felt comfortable having another serve me and I would not start now. Besides, I had to think of Edweene. If another were to accompany me on my foolhardy rides, I might lose my most trusted ally. For she would certainly have no interest in hanging about if there was even the slightest chance that another might discover her true nature.

As I stood, unbuckling my armor, something in the darkness shifted. "The shadowy knight speaks true," a woman's voice spooked me. I stepped back against the door behind me. The voice was firm, having none of the lilt that court etiquette demanded of ladies back home. Within a breath, I knew that it was Edweene—my oft-times companion.

"I did not know you awaited me here, my lady. I thought you had gone about your business when I did not see your blasted bird."

Edweene rarely came into towns with me, afraid of the implications if an abbot or knight might discover her secret. Edweene was a Lych. And a Lych is an undead abomination to The Temple and The God. I struggled mightily with her presence on occasion, even though she'd saved me—both physically and in the context of my Soul—more than once.

I had great discomfort with the fact that she had perished beneath my own knife more than two years prior and was kept alive only by the containment of her Soul in the Phylactery that was embedded in the ring she wore.

Any knight sworn to The God would be obliged to smite her, destroy the vessel that held her Soul, and send it to its eternal resting place. I, on the other hand, had tried desperately to make allowances for a woman of ruthlessness, wisdom, and deadliness in combat.

As my eyes adjusted, I saw her. She sat on the edge of my bed, her scimitar on her lap, sharpening stone in her off-hand. Her straw-colored hair was braided tightly against the sides of her head, and her eyes glowed dimly blue in the darkness—I sometimes thought she could control their fire and sometimes worried they were indicative of her mood.

"Nevertheless," she said. "My blasted bird, as you say, watched you from the night. You lack the skills of observation to notice her. It was important for me to talk to you, to tell you my thoughts. So, I took a risk." I stepped back away from her, as was my instinct. I was still uncomfortable with her nature, and what it might mean. I was, after all, a child of The God, raised to view the living dead as hateful creatures of the Devil. Overcoming one's childhood predilections, it seems, is much harder than it should be. My back pressed against the door. She smiled wryly at me. She knew my heart better than any—perhaps even better than my sister. "Do not be a fool on this," she said.

"My Crusade no longer takes me against the heathen. I believe that The God has identified for me a greater threat to his glory," I said. "My Crusade is for truth, the darkness within our own camp—against whoever betrayed me in the woods that night. He is the bigger threat, for he is a disease in The God's own body," I said to her. Even as I said it, I felt the sticky arrogance in the statement, as though I was The God's chosen.

She knew what had happened on that dark, rainy night. She'd even been the one that had pointed it out to me. I secured her eyes with mine but could not hold her long; they still disturbed me. I still often had visions of the life slipping from them as I murdered her two and more years ago. She knew this and avoided locking gazes

with me, mostly—unless she wanted to make a
point.

"I understand, Aaron. But you are sometimes
a self-obsessed idiot. Your inability to focus on
naught but your petty grievances clouds your
mind," she said.

"You wound me," I said jokingly, trying—and
failing—to make light of a conversation I was uncomfortable having.

"This is no matter for jokes," she said, her blue
eyes flashing. She slid the blade of her curved
sword along the stone, the sound grinding my
teeth. "You know the Tartans," she continued.
"This boy will be tortured unto death. And what
if this stranger speaks the truth—what if he was
ordered there by the king or bishop? What then?
Do you not see where this could help you on your
fool's quest?"

"I see nothing but a trap."

"Where is the fool conscience of the man I
sought out to save me—the man that risked his
life to fight a sorcerer of great power?" She rose
from the bed and slid her sword into its scabbard.

"Where is the heartless murderer that meant to skewer two helpless concubines?" I asked, my voice full of venom, driven, I am sure, by my own guilt.

Edweene cast me a single glance that flashed angry cobalt in the darkness.

"The ruthless murderer is still here, but your conscience disappears when it is most needed. Very well, Chosen of The God. But do not forget your conscience, it controls your soul. And more over do not forget that the Sixth Tenant of your God is Humility. I have no such tenant."

Edweene stepped into the cool night and disappeared, as she was wont to do.

"My conscience is still being sated," I whispered into the dark.

CHAPTER 3
THE BREAKING STAR

I started for Clurak early in the morning, knowing it would be a long ride. The Pilgrim's Approach lay more than a hundred miles to the Southwest, and the nights were getting cold and dark. The campaigning season was long over and would not return until spring. Soon, winter's storms would come, and more rain would fall upon the Holy Land. This would give me much needed time to pursue my betrayer.

The morning started ominously colder than the land was wont, and it was crisp and clear—rain clouds typical for this time of year were nowhere in sight. But, I knew this land. Un-

predictable winds could bring winter thunder-
heads in from the sea with no warning, and I
gained no confidence from the dark, clear skies. I
had considered making the trek to Clurak by Sea.
But, my last experience on the Sea of Sorrows
had been somewhat less than confidence-inspir-
ing. And with storms being a true possibility, I
was not stirred to journey in such a way. I would
ride, I decided. The sea was for other men than
me.

As I began my journey, Edweene's rebuke was
fresh in my mind, eating away at my insides.
My heart *did* ache for the young knight, but I
had to pursue my singular goal. My thirst for
vengeance was unquenchable and undeniable. It
was inevitable that I would turn something up, if
indeed Gavreaux was true to his word and had
sent missive to his agents in Clurak to help me.
This knight, Prenot, would die at the hands of the
Tartans. His sacrifice was not lost on me, and I
would honor him for it, by ensuring the fall of my
enemies—traitors to The God.

My horse's shoes clopped loudly on the
hard-packed road as I rode south and west. In-

termittent cottonwood and oak, thrust upward
from the thick, briars that bordered the road,
like twisted, white pillars, giving the thoroughfare
the appearance of a great, uncovered hallway. I
kept the beast's pace steady, careful not to wind
the creature. It would be a long ride. The next
way station was a hundred miles distant where
this ancient road, constructed a thousand years
past by the engineers of the Empire of Travanah,
met the Pilgrim's Approach. Just a mile west of
there, the estate of Lord Duveaux, a Thayne in
the service of Earl Richeau, straddled the great
road. Pilgrimages would often stop there and
take advantage of the old knight's hospitality. He
was well known and well respected in the Holy
Land, and I intended to sojourn there in two
nights hence. It was the first of such places that
would take me along my route to the capital.

The first night, I made camp beside the imperial road, Edweene's strange raven perched in
an ancient and ratty cottonwood above me, its
blue-glittering eyes staring down as though it
waited for me to shut my eyes before it feasted
on me. I started a fire, disconcerted by the crea-

ture's presence. After a quick meal of hardtack and cheese, I wrapped myself in my bedroll and leaned against the great tree's trunk. I stayed awake for some time but drifted as the sliver of moon rose to mid-of-night. Sometime in the early morning, the sound of armored hooves pounded past me on the road and woke me from my slumber. My fire had turned to naught but embers, and I slid toward the road as quietly as a woodland creature. There was nothing there. The rider had passed. It must have been a knight or cavalryman on the way to Clurak or any number of places between. I slinked back to my place against the tree and leaned my head back. Nowhere could I see the raven then. I drifted to sleep once again.

The next day, I woke to the sound of birdsong and the rustling of leaves in the early morning breeze. The raven was perched on a nearby branch, its gaze fixed upon me as I went about my morning routines. I broke my fast with a meager meal of dried fruit and salted meat, washing it down with water from my skin. The road stretched out before me, an uncomfortably straight path through the twisted woods, and I set off at a steady pace, the raven following along in spurts and starts between trees, where it would fly ahead and perch until I passed and then the same again, and again. Each time, its black wings caught the air in flashes and snaps, bringing my eyes to it as though it goaded me.

As the sun climbed higher in the sky, the heat of the day began to take its toll. I stopped to rest in the shade of a twisted oak, the raven alighting on a low-hanging branch. It watched me with those unsettling blue eyes as I tended to my horse and checked my supplies. I couldn't shake the feeling that the creature was more than just a simple bird and held some deeper purpose or meaning. With a shake of my head, I mounted up and continued my way.

The following night, I camped beside a bubbling stream, the water cool and clear. I refilled my skin and washed the dust of the road from my face and hands. The raven perched on a rock nearby, its head cocked to the side as if listening to the sounds of the night. I built a small fire and huddled close to its warmth, my thoughts turning to the task ahead. The bishop's betrayal weighed heavily on my mind, as it always did, and the long days gave me little to think about but vengeance. As I drifted to sleep, the raven's eyes glinted in the firelight, a silent guardian watching over me—and a convicting reminder of Egweene's judgments.

The next day, I rode on, the landscape changing from thorny forests to rolling hills and back again. The raven was my constant companion, a shadow on the wind that followed me wherever I went. At times, I found myself talking to the creature, sharing my thoughts and fears as if it could understand. And perhaps it could, for there was an intelligence in those blue eyes that seemed almost human. Perhaps the nun listened.

On the third day, I crested a hill and could see in the distance where the flattening of the land and the lightening of the wood. I knew that I was nearing my destination, that the end of my journey was close—at least the Pilgrim's approach, which would take me to Devreaux's estate and then onward to Clurak. I spurred my horse onward, the raven bounding between thorny, wasted oaks as if leading the way. The road grew more well-traveled, and I passed signs of merchants and pilgrims making their way to and from the Approach Road, here the trail was getting well-worn. I kept my head down and my hand on my sword, watchful for signs of trouble. But the Road would all have to wait. The day was getting long, and I had no desire to travel at night. I'd reach it tomorrow.

As evening approached, I found a secluded spot off the road to camp. I tethered my horse and set about gathering firewood, the raven watching from its perch in a nearby tree. The night was cold and clear, the stars shining brightly overhead. I sat beside the fire, sharpening my blade and thinking of the trials to come. I knew that I would need all my strength and cunning to face the challenges ahead, but I was ready. As things were going, the sword was the least on my mind. I had no idea how I'd deal with the politics of Clurak—how I'd confront the bishop or find evidence of his unholy deceit. I was lost here. Lost. And, on that thought, and with a final glance at the raven, I lay down to rest, my mind filled with thoughts of vengeance and justice and having no idea how I'd achieve any of it.

The gloaming found me packing and preparing to go. I cinched the saddle to my steed and affixed my bedroll to its cantle. After donning my leather armor, I slipped on the green surcoat that bore the River and Lion of Riverdale—in the case that some knight or Crusader might happen upon me—and then belted on sword and knives. Over it all, I tied my heavy cloak to keep out the wet and chill. I led my mount out upon the road and climbed into the saddle.

It was still nearly dark in the twilight hours when I started the day. The morning was colder than yesterday and the night lasted well into the morning. I figured that evening would find me at the Pilgrim's Approach crossroads. From there it was a short jaunt to Ser Duveaux's estate where I could have another warm meal and perhaps a bed somewhat softer than the earth. I was getting soft, I realized, when I craved such things. I had returned to the Holy Land in search of adventure and danger—a return to times when my life had stood upon a dagger's edge. Now, had I lost that desire? Had it been replaced with a single minded vengeance, in the comfortable places of Clurak?

The day wore on. Still, I saw no sign of Edweene or her raven. I began to worry over their absence. A full day was unlike her and I wondered if I had upset her or disappointed her such that she might abandon my quest. The idea sat in my mind and nagged at me. Was it this perceived anger with me or my guilt that caused the discomfiture? As darkness began to claim the land, I smelled death. It came to me first in small wafts of sickly sweet air carried upon the breeze. But, as I continued onward, the smell ripened, thickened in my nose.

My horse shied, whinnied its nervousness. I felt its anxiety in my own heart. I calmed her, brushing and patting my hand across her neck, whispering soft soothing things in her ear. The reassurance I knew was as much for me as her. The beast stilled and pranced a bit sideways. I too stilled, calmed, turned in the saddle to look ahead as she pranced about.

Perhaps two hundred paces ahead on the left, a single orange lantern burned in a covered sconce, casting out a bloody orange shadow play that danced ominously on the road ahead. There too, I saw the broad cobble of the Pilgrim's Approach, dark and flickering in the lantern light. Faint sounds of iron mechanics, un-oiled and squeaking, drifted to my ears. I swung myself from the saddle and led my horse from the road. Leaving her behind, I crept ahead, keeping to the thick brush on the left side of the road. I drew my sword and knife as I got closer to cross-roads, and reduced my already slow advance. I watched the trees on all sides as I moved ahead, toe-heel, toe-heel. It took some time, but soon I arrived at the perimeter of the spooky orange lantern light. I crouched there in the darkness and waited, listening.

The sound of creaking iron was much louder there—something turning, a wheel or gear or the like. I heard nothing else, but my breathing, and my heart pattering lightly in my chest. I was calm, expectant—the calmness that often took me before combat had settled upon me; my senses were sharp and ready. I wished that Edweene was with me to watch my flanks or back—or even to deal with whatever threat may be ahead, but I had not seen her since she stormed from my room at the Stone, nor had I seen the raven that harbingered her presence. I could do nothing for that now. Steeling myself, I carefully parted the brush and gingerly moved toward the strange sound.

The smell of death grew stronger until it was all consuming. A body smells a certain way when it has been exposed to the open air for a day or two—this one was not uniquely putrid, but I had not expected it here. It was a smell I'd experienced a hundred times, but one I would never get used to. I breathed deeply through my mouth, and continued ahead. The sound grew closer, the squeaking now almost unbearable. The light from the lantern grew brighter and warmer. Finally, I reached the brush that bordered the crossroads. I stopped momentarily and listened closely again. Again, I heard nothing but that infernal scraping sound. The only consolation was:

if anyone waited for me, they could hear nothing of my approach.

With that thought giving me confidence, I parted the brush. Ten paces ahead of me, my eyes beheld a terrible sight. Several paces from the crossroads on a cleared site of hardened heart, a large wooden device, circular, like a wagon's wheel, was set upon a wooden mount by a metal axle. The internal spokes of the wheel were shaped in the Five-Pointed Star of The God. A weathered dais was raised next to it to assist an executioner—or more accurately, a torturer—in affixing a condemned soul to what was known as the Breaking Star. There, he would chain the prisoner down, spread out—head to the top point of the Star, and limbs to each other point—and spin him round. As the condemned spun, the executioner would crush his limbs with a heavy mallet. His broken body would then be left to die as food for the buzzards—a spectacle used throughout the Holy Land in places of great traffic as deterrents to those indigenous peasants and others who might speak or act against The God. It was a technique that I thought counterproductive, but who was I to question the ways of The God?

On this particular Breaking Star was strapped the body of a man. He was bloated, his exposed skin, graying and tearing and splitting. Putrid gasses and odors rose from the corpse and filled the air with its horror. But, this man was no peasant or infidel, Broken on the Star by the Holy Temple or its soldiers. This man wore the colors of House Duveaux—a gray field behind a single Star, above a green pine—on his surcoat. His long hair drifted in the breeze with the motion of the wheel which rocked back and forth, its iron axle creaking and squeaking with the movement. The blood below had long since been absorbed into the earth and was now nothing but an oily dark spot.

It struck me then that I remembered seeing the Breaking Star on my way to the Stone. But, it had been empty on my journey here, no tortured soul chained upon it. Someone had done this recently—within the last two days. I wondered if it had something to do with the rider that I'd heard last night. Wary of ambush, I crept back into the brush and watched. After some time, I thought it safe and stepped out into the clearing. I strode to the wheel, reached out and stopped it with my hand. The metallic squeaking ceased and I secured it with a piece of rope that I found dangling from the Star. I now got a clear look at the dead man. His body was too rotted and I could not identify him. He wore a gray beard that hung limply from his decaying face, and was caked with days-old blood. His legs and arms were shattered where a hammer had crushed bone, torn muscle and ripped sinew apart. His face held the deep, bloody scars of a scourge. His surcoat was cut open between star and pine, and his armor creased from a pounding he'd obviously taken from a heavy, blunt weapon.

A parchment was tacked to his throat by a crossbow bolt. It waved and crackled in the breeze. I reached for it, but had to step back. Odors so awful rose from his corpse that I was forced to step away and cover my face. Once again, I forced myself forward and tore the message from his rancid neck, stepping quickly away lest I retch.

Once I was twenty paces distant, I opened the parchment and read the contents within. It was written in the scrolling hand of the Gol, but in the language of The God. It read:

Savior of Clurak:

I know that you believe that your heart serves The God. But, he has no place for you. You shall save no more, and you shall only offend those you wish to serve. Abandon your quest and retire to your home, lest disaster takes you and The God moves against you as it has moved against your man Duveaux. All those that follow you shall perish, all those that assist you shall perish, and the knight, Prenot shall die regardless. The God wills it. The Old Gods demand it. Only darkness awaits you on your path. This war between the Faithful and the Crusaders shall not be abated.

-- The Tawl

I carefully folded up the parchment and slipped it into my belt pouch. Whoever had written this missive mistakenly assumed that I was headed to save Ser Prenot. Or did they assume that he was part of a bigger picture—my bigger quest? There was some evidence here that the knight, Prenot, played into some misbegotten assumption on the part of the killer. And who was The Tawl? All these things, I considered, as I fetched my steed and brought her to the Star. I had to move quickly because the dead knight on the Star set a terrible expectation for what I might find Duveaux's manor, to which I had wanted to ride and sojourn.

If there was death awaiting me there, I wanted to get on with it.

Once I had returned to the Star, I tethered her. She was nervous around the body, skittish, and found it better to put the tree to which I had tethered her between her and the rancid corpse. I didn't blame her. If I could have, I'd have been gone from that wicked place. But, the knight deserved burial. And so, I broke the chains that bound him, and set to burying him under a pile of stones—it was the best I could do.

"The God take him, please," I whispered as I carried the final stone and heaped it upon his makeshift cairn. It was the only prayer he would get from me—or likely anyone. *How sad to die out here with no one to care for him*, I thought. But, it was a fleeting thought. This knight was one of thousands in such a situation.

It was time for me to ride on. Ser Duveaux would either need my help, or he need burying.

Chapter 4

Duveaux's Estate

An hour later, I sat atop my charger on a low hill overlooking Duveaux's estate. It was deep night; what light had remained of dusk was gone. The estate looked like a haunted place. A smattering of orange lanterns and braziers glowed dimly at various spots around the grounds—concentrated near the central manor. The manor house itself was a square, clay structure of only two levels—just what was befitting a low-born knight in the Holy Land. On the second level, a balcony protruded, its doorway open to the night. Candles burned within, casting its banister in hazy, wavering yellow light. Deeper within the grounds, the black outlines of a stable and small barrack could be seen against the night's horizon. Not designed as a castle, the estate had a low wall, perhaps eight feet tall, ringing the entire place.

The ring of stone and clay stretched for a thousand paces, bordering the Pilgrim's Approach and another thousand paces deep. In a siege, it would be easily breached. It was designed merely to keep bandits at bay and foraging animals from getting to the crops and livestock within. A gate stood at the end of a short, hard-packed way that sliced perpendicular to the Pilgrim's Approach. Two lanterns hung at the gate, some eight hundred paces distant, like fiery red embers, rocking gently in the breeze.

A sharp tickle of nervousness rose in the pit of my belly. The place was silent and felt dead. I led my horse off the road and dismounted. I would walk in from here. I made my way along the wall, keeping low, behind the brush, such as it was. Still, my right side was exposed to the emptiness of the road, the sparse bushes providing little cover. Anyone from that side would have an easy time lacing a crossbow bolt through my heart. I tried not to think of such things and forged ahead. Midway along the side of the estate, I decided to scale the wall instead of entering through the gate. If enemies waited within, I'd rather come at them across the grounds than through the gate.

It was a simple thing to pull myself up and over the wall. I landed on a walkway that was elevated a foot or two from the ground, just enough to give archers or crossbowmen room to loose their arrows and bolts over the battlement. It was dark on the inside of the wall—the lanterns' bullseye being directed outwards to detect intruders. I was instantly more comfortable, my natural state being one of stealth. I settled for a moment to let my eyes adjust. Once that was done, I stepped off the walkway to squat among a patch of thick briars.

A few hundred paces away, the outer wall of the manor was illuminated by a single lantern and the dim light from the open balcony. That was where I was headed. The trick was getting there undetected, but the darkness was my friend. I waited and watched. There was no movement, but I knew—in the pit of my belly—that there was something there. This was some sort of trap. It would not dissuade me from finding out if there was anyone left within.

I began my stalk. Slowly, deliberately, I flitted between the darkest parts of the grounds, avoiding anywhere that light might find its way from a lantern, candle, or moon above. I stole ahead towards the manor house. I was deathly silent, a skill that I had honed for years as a Dark Man—the trained assassins put to work by the king during the Third Crusade. In no time, I had picked my way to the wall. On my way to the manor, I crept through a well-kept, if recently crushed, garden of corn, tomato, and beans. The body of a young worker lay in the smashed-down rows, his body but a lump of cold flesh. I continued on, gooseflesh spreading across my skin.

I soon reached a well that stood near the end of the garden and halfway to the house. The raised granite and sandstone well was three feet high and covered with a small A-framed structure. I crouched behind it and peered toward the manor. I rested my hand atop it and felt something wet and dark. Pulled my hand back quickly, I brought it to my face to see what was there—dark liquid and thick—most likely blood. The attackers had probably thrown bodies down the well to hide them or render the water un-drinkable.

I scooted along the side of the well, careful to avoid the blood and not make a sound. At last, I had a better look at the building. Silence. I began to feel like maybe I was wrong. Perhaps there would be no one waiting in ambush. Per-haps the point was made on the Breaking Star. I moved ahead slowly, keeping at a crouch. My eyes moved constantly, scanning the grounds for ambush, and keeping appraised of the situation at the manor. Was there an archer on the roof or on the balcony? A swordsman waiting in ambush in the weeds nearby?

In long moments, I arrived at the low wall sur-rounding the manor house. I was surprised that no one had attempted to ambush me on the grounds. If I was to assassinate someone here, an arrow feathered into them as they traversed across the grounds would have been my first choice: no close-in work and lots of empty space. I reached up and grasped the top of the wall, ready to flip myself over and into the grounds proper when I heard a noise on the far side of the wall. It sounded like boots scraping on tiles. Carefully, I eased myself up the wall until I could see over the top. Inside, a lantern lit the small courtyard. Across twenty paces of grass and stone walkways, the manor house doorway yawned, its door hanging from broken hinges. Yellow candlelight flickered out from there and the balcony above. There was no one on the balcony, no one in the doorway. But, on the walkway, midway to the corner of the manse, a man crouched, his crossbow leveled at the front gate on the other side of the building.

I'd make short work of this one. I chanced a quick glance about to verify my initial findings. Seeing no one, I hefted myself quietly onto the top of the wall. I slid silently down the far side to drop onto soft dirt among the well-manicured brush. I crouched there and watched my nemesis for a long moment. He was fidgety. He knew someone was around but did not expect me to be behind him. His attention was transfixed by something or someone on the other side of the building. I stole ahead, sliding along like a serpent. Two steps, three steps, four, and I was upon him. Before he even sensed I was there, my knife slid across his throat, my other hand holding his head back so he would die more easily, more silently. I helped him slip silently to the ground, dead, careful that my eyes did not meet his—for the souls of my kills still haunted me. I peered ahead to discover what he might be looking at but saw nothing—or was there a brief flutter of movement in the night? I watched for a breath more and decided it was nothing.

As quietly as possible, I slid his body along the pathway and stashed it in the bushes. Once I had disguised it behind thick hedges, I turned my attention back to the matter at hand. I crept along the wall until I reached the opened doorway. Keeping close to the wall, I slid to my knees and peered around the corner into the manor house.

The doorway was two broad doors wide. The heavy, wood and iron-bound doors hung, broken, from iron hinges designed to keep attackers at bay. The entry room was large and empty save a cracked and savaged central table that once held some sculpture, now shattered on the tile floor. A stairway swept up and out of the room to a loft above. A doorway to the right and one to the left gave egress from the room. The bodies of two men lay in the room—one lay in the center, sprawled over the busted table, and one lay mid-way up the stairs—crossbow bolts embedded in their chests, necks, and backs.

I quickly checked the bottom floor and found no one alive. Two Gol warriors were laid low in the manor dining room, and a third, I found broken by a mace or cudgel to the skull in the kitchen. They were Tartans, I assumed. I knew them by their war god's Black Fist, sewn on red disc and worn as a device on their surcoats. The heathens still worshiped the Old Gods—and these ones bent at the altar of their most violent one, though I wondered if it was any more terrifying than our own.

Soon, I found the manor's native cook, killed by a curved knife to her neck, lying beside the Tartan in a pool of day-old blood. I found nothing else on the first floor and returned to the staircase, moving quickly and stealthily. Where there was one Gol, there were bound to be scores. I had found three dead Golish knights—known as Sanahen—and a crossbowman: a strange mix to be traveling together. Mostly, Gols fought as cohesive units of Sanahen or other lesser men and women-at-arms, like archers or infantry. I derived this must be some special group—a strike force on a Golish War Hunt—special missions of great significance. It told me they were likely well-trained, experienced zealots.

I took the stairs quickly, sacrificing some stealth for the desire to be off the damn things as quickly as possible. When I reached the small loft, one archway opened to my left and another to my right. I crouched again and listened. My heart beat loudly, pulsing in my ears. My breath was short and rapid. The absence of motion was nerve-wracking. The room that was attached to the balcony, which I had seen from outside, was to my left. I worried my back would be exposed, but I had no options. I'd done all I could to clear the bottom floor of enemies so no one would be coming from down there. Unless, of course, more were outside. I ignored that nagging thought. I could do nothing about it. Survival favored the bold, so I crept toward the left and prayed no enemy lurked to my rear. Yellow light flickered and danced, illuminating the edge of the door in strange, wavering shadows. As I approached the opening, I heard the smallest movement, a minute shifting—sniffling, or re-aligning—within. I slipped to the door. I reached the archway and slid my head around just enough to see within.

The God bestowed providence upon me, for the light was behind them and darkness behind me. It struck me odd that the warriors who had delivered this kind of death on experienced knights would wait for me in such a foolish position. They waited in ambush, facing the balcony that they obviously thought I would scale. One man was hooded and held a crossbow; the other waited with his scimitar drawn, prepared to rush forward and kill me as I hung from the balcony's rail. The crossbowman was closer, not ten paces away. The other was near twenty, on the other side of a bed, whose legs and frame were cracked and busted, linens all unkempt. Upon the bed, twisted up in the linens, the tortured remains of Lady Duveaux lay, broken and naked.

My enemies knew that I was close or would not be as prepared as they were, but they did not expect me to come from behind. The candlelight flickered as a slight breeze laced through the room. Tongues of darkness licked out at me as one candle went out and the others guttered and struggled to stay lit. I readied myself and steeled my nerves. As I prepared to bring these men to their Gods, I heard a noise below—a scraping or sliding across the floor. I considered delaying my attack, but I'd have to deal with it sometime. Now, I had the surprise. I hoped I'd be finished in time to deal with this new threat when I was finished.

I slipped ahead, intent on the crossbow wielder first. I led with my free hand, my other holding my long knife; my sword was sheathed, its length a liability in this scenario. As I arrived in striking distance of the crossbowman, I reached ahead with my free hand to grab his head and pull it back, exposing his throat. As I did, I realized, concealed beneath his cloak and hood, he wore a mail coif that covered his gullet. But my hands were already in motion. I cursed myself a fool as I wrenched back his head, my knife sliding harmlessly across his armored throat. He dropped his crossbow and cried out, struggling against me. He lashed his hands backward in a vain attempt to free himself. I didn't give him much time to live, however, as I drove the blade of my knife through his eye, yanked it out, and drove it in again. The man fell to the floor, his one undamaged eye staring up at me, dead and dark and filled with fear. I swallowed my remorse and turned toward my other target. He was already moving.

The second Gol launched himself over the broken bed toward me, his sword held aloft in both hands to cleave me in two. It was a mistake, one for which I was prepared for. But he was faster than I had imagined, and I had to backpedal and struggle to get my knife up to deflect his sword in time. Fortunately, when he stepped upon the bedframe, it broke and split apart again under his weight. He stumbled, caught himself, and continued the charge. But, his attack had been delayed just enough. I had my knife raised in time to send his sword sidelong, but the impact vibrated through my arm and pitched me off balance. I caught myself as I lurched backward, drawing my broadsword as I did. His dark eyes, visible behind his visor, narrowed angrily, and he circled to his right, my left. I followed his lead, circling right, my knife ahead and sword behind, ready to slash when given the opportunity.

He was impetuous, well trained but impatient. It was evident from his first charge. He came in hard, his blade descending almost too quickly. I dodged sideways and merely pushed it further aside with the crosspiece of my knife. He spun sideways, sweeping his sword around in a horizontal arch that was designed to cut me down. But, I stepped in too quickly and drove my sword through the armor plating on his ribs, the blade slipping between riveted plates, and cutting a rift of bloody mess through his side. He flopped backwards but maintained a grip on his weapon.

He forced himself to stand, favoring his undamaged right side, his left hand grasping the wound on his ribs. Blood pumped through his fingers. He knew he was already dead. I could see it in the curvature of his eyes, deep inside his visor. He staggered once and then lurched forward. As he clumsily came at me, I finished him with my knife through his gorge. But his momentum carried him through, and his blade slid across my left thigh, opening the skin to the air.

I sheathed my knife, grasped my leg, and squeezed, hoping to keep the light flow of blood from becoming a gush. I prodded the downed man with my blade, verifying his expiration. Blood pooled rapidly under him, expanding into a crimson lake. I stepped away, trying to keep my boots clean from it. How foolish, I thought, that in all this death, I worried over the soles of my boots. I suppressed the lump that worked its way into my throat, the need to cry out at needless death. There was still work to do. Then, I heard a loud scraping noise behind me, followed by the sound of iron-shod boots on clay tiles. I spun to face the door through which I had come.

A third Gol stepped out of the shadows then, beneath the archway. The noise I had heard from downstairs? Another large, dark shadow loomed behind him, black in the gray darkness behind. I assumed the shadow was a trick of the light—I was tired and wounded, panting from the exertion of killing the last two Golish warriors. So, my mind was not wholly clear. The third knight was tall, and broad of shoulder. He wore a full-faced helmet that ended below his eyes. A mail veil hung below it, protecting the face and neck. He was wrapped in steel and wore a heavy, curved falchion on one side and a curved dirk on the other. How he moved so silently, encased in all that steel, was beyond me. He was obviously the leader of this War Hunt.

"I would prefer not to kill you, Crusader," he said as he stood there, brave as shite, his gravelly voice muffled behind his armored veil. I thought I recognized it from somewhere, somewhere distant and forgotten. A fool's notion, really. I'd never faced such a man. He moved sideways, gripping the pommel of a long, curved falchion. "You have already killed my soldiers, and that has angered me plenty. But, those I serve would prefer you not perish here in your lands."

"Who are you?"

"I am the Tawl," he said.

"The Tawl? And what might that be?" I asked in my most sarcastic voice. I stepped a little forward. "You have killed my lord Duveaux and his retainers. You have massacred his people. What should prevent me from killing you now, as I have your men-at-arms?"

He laughed at that, which was somewhat disconcerting since I had just dispatched two of his knights. "You, kill me?" he asked when he'd finished with his guffaw. "You could not hope to kill me. I am the Tawl."

I swallowed and breathed deep, using the break to catch my breath and nurse my wounded leg. "Then, tell me, Tawl," I started, "who do you serve?"

"I killed your knight Duveaux—the owner of this . . ." he swept his hands wide, ". . . insult to the people of Clurak, and we feasted on his bones," the man said and then added, "I, too, broke his man on the Star." His smile widened.

It was feral and filled with hate, eyes narrowed. "It was gratifying," he hissed.

I stepped toward him. "You shall perish for your murders," I said.

"Murders? And what are your killings, Dark Man?" he asked, twisting the last words.

The Tawl stepped aside and the shadow behind him shifted once and then surged forward into the room. I was forced to step back and gasp as a massive man-thing, a foot taller than the tallest man I'd ever witnessed—so tall he had to bend to fit beneath the tall archway—strode into the room. The beast-man was heavily muscled. It was two heads taller than a normal man when it stood tall. Spiked, black hair covered its body in intermittent clusters. A row of finger-long black spikes ran the length of its spine from skull to tailbone, where a short, barbed tail swung dangerously behind it. It raised its head to peer at me, eyes empty, black and filled with rage. It's jagged, wolf-like mouth was pulled up in a hungry smile. It gripped a massive two-headed hammer in its taloned hands.

A Gorgon.

I'd heard of them, but I'd never seen one. Once, half-a-hundred years past, an army of the creatures invaded the kingdoms of Bannon and Rogga from the Firewall Peaks. The two countries had combined armies to put down the ravaging tribes. Since then, it had been rumored that Gorgon mercenaries sometimes served as shock troops for Golish armies, having somehow traversed the Sea of Sorrows to Gol Toran. But those were stories. No one that I knew had ever really remembered seeing them.

The beast would not find me an easy foe. I turned toward it and set myself for its attack, my long knife held before me and my broadsword behind, ready to strike.

"You die now, Crusader!" the thing hissed out in a deep, garbled language I could scarcely understand.

Then the man-creature raised its hammer above its head and swept toward me, slavering, and growling as it came.

Chapter 5
Gorgon

The Gorgon charged and swung its maul—an enormous arching swing crashed into a beam that supported the manor's roof. I ducked under the weapon as the building shook, and the beam shattered, sending particles of clay and splinters of wood spraying in all directions. I rotated away from it, my sword sliding across its armored leg as I did. It failed to penetrate but drew the beast-man's attention enough to dissuade another such attack. It howled at me and retreated a step.

I worked my way backward, watching helplessly as the Tawl leaped from the balcony behind, escaping into the night. I wanted that man's blood. But I had more pressing matters to deal with.

The Gorgon came in again; this time, it was more careful, advancing slowly, its hammer held in a ready position, looking for me to make a mistake. Ignoring my leg for the moment, gritting through the rising pain. I waited, circling to the left as it approached, keeping as much pressure off my wounded leg as I might. It let the head of its hammer waver a little as if it was dropping it. I concluded that it was trying to lure me in—someone this size could not already be exhausted, no matter the size of its hammer. I did not fall for the bait. I choked back my aggression, thinking it better to wait for this stronger fighter out or trick it into attacking. I continued my circle, having now rotated such that my longer sword was ahead, tip pointed at its heart, forcing it to keep its distance, and my knife held behind, ready to lunge.

It let out a snort, and what appeared to be impatience etched on the narrowed eyes and bared fangs. I smiled and waved it forward with the tip of my sword. It was only too happy to oblige as it batted it aside with its hand and pushed forward. I leaned into its attack, and thrust forward with my knife, putting all my strength behind it.

The blade punched forward into its abdomen plates and skinned off to the side, barely slowing its charge. My momentum carried me forward, under the arch of its hammer which caught me in a glancing blow on my buttocks as I pushed past it. Its strength was such that it propelled me, face-first, into the broken bed frame behind it. Knowing it would be on me in no time, I rolled onto my back and struggled to my feet.

I was almost too late, as the creature came on aggressively. I dodged away, staggering to my right as the hammer crashed down on the broken corpse of Lady Duveaux, crushing through what remained of her and shattering the bedframe. I staggered forward now, leading with my knife, which I was beginning to realize did not have the weight to penetrate either its armor or its natural hide. And so it was again, as the blade slid off of the creature's forearm. But, this time I spun after the deflection and brought my sword down on its shoulder and felt the bone there give. The man-creature howled again, stood tall and sneered at me, spittle dripping from its jaws.

I was exhausted, the fight nearly out of me. My armor and sword were heavy, not designed for lengthy melees. I stood and faced him, my heart pounding, my breath coming in short, deep gasps. My enemy appeared barely winded; the yellow-orange lights made him appear as some otherworldly demon. "I shall kill you, Gorgon," I said flatly, between breaths, doing my best to appear as though I was not beginning to break.

It smiled at me. "No, Crusader, I shall kill you and then feast on your bones as I have those around you." Its voice was hollow, deep, and filled with rage. It continued, "You shall not see your knight again. He is ours, as are his secrets."

"You speak of secrets," I said, trying to buy time, gather my breath, my strength. "What secrets?"

"You know. Fool. That is why you seek to rescue him. Now, enough talk. You are near to death, Crusader. Time to feel my hammer."

It rushed forward. But I was ready since it telegraphed its attack with the tone of its voice. I pitched forward and left. The hammer skimmed across my shoulder, not damaging me at all but sending me off balance. I spun around, my back turned toward him. I dived to the ground—an attempt to avoid the follow-on strike that I knew would be coming. Without a lucky miss, I knew I was done for. No strike came. I turned and arose clumsily in a ready position.

Just then, there was another voice in the room, deep and threatening. "It is my turn to face you, creature." Behind the Gorgon, a knight came though the archway into the bed chamber. His steel gleamed in the low light, and his surcoat and shield bore the two Stars and Horse's head of Ser Richeau. He wore a full-faced helmet and carried his shield before him, heavy broadsword ready for the attack.

I breathed a sigh of relief and a prayer to The God.

The Gorgon twisted to face this new threat and swung its hammer at my new ally with a great shriek. The knight raised his shield and absorbed the massive strike. The knight staggered backward and fell to a knee, the face of his shield deformed and bent, but still serviceable. He raised his own broadsword and pushed himself back up, rushing forward with a howl. The creature thrust the hammer forward to meet the charge, but the knight showed great agility in his steel and dodged sideways away from it, swinging his sword down to slice across the creature's back.

The man-beast growled and knocked the knight aside with a throw of its fist. It faced him again and raised its hammer for a killing blow as the knight raised his busted-up shield again. Now ignored by the Gorgon warrior, I rushed forward and slashed my blade across the top of its exposed heel. My blade split the tendon, and its leg collapsed under its weight.

The creature dropped its hammer and lurched forward onto the floor. It was not done. It rolled onto its back and thrust itself upon its good leg. Glaring at me, it lashed out at me with its taloned hand and roared hatred into the night. With what strength remained with me, I dodged underneath its clumsy attack and drilled my sword through the thick hide on its abdomen. It kicked out at me with its dead foot, hammering me backward, just as the knight's sword came down on its head, embedding into its hardened skull.

The Gorgon leaned forward, let out a blood-filled gasp, and ceased moving.

I strode haltingly to the motionless form and kicked it, keeping my sword pointed at its split head as if anything could survive such a stroke. The knight wrenched out his weapon. Blood and bone spattered across my leg. I sneered thankfully at the man as he removed his helmet.

"I think it is dead." I knew the voice immediately. He was the shadowy figure from outside the barrack at The Stone.

"You followed me from the Stone."

"Not exactly. I passed you on the road from the Stone. One night out. I expected to sojourn here, as is normal upon this road. I decided to meet you here and speak to you under Lord Duveaux's roof. I've been waiting for a day."

"Then you saw—"

"It was already done, and so was the killing at the Breaking Star. I would have engaged the enemy when I arrived, but there were too many. Knowing you were likely coming, I decided that I had a better chance fighting the heathen murderers together." He must have seen my skeptical look and quickly added, "There is little honor in getting one's self butchered."

"Then, you let me come in here and face these shite eaters alone?"

The knight seemed taken aback as if I were questioning his courage. It was, in fact, the case.

"I did not know you were here, my lord. I waited beyond the gate. It seems you went over the wall, further back, where I could not observe you." The man's explanation seemed lacking. But I could not question the fact that his arrival likely saved my life. I was about to respond when another voice came from behind me, near the balcony through which the self-proclaimed Tawl had escaped.

"I took down two more by the billet and watched as another fled." It was Edweene.

I turned toward her voice. She perched upon the balcony in her leather armor, hair pulled back in a braid, face hidden in the shadows of the night. Her eyes glittered cobalt and bright in the darkness—the hue they had when she'd just finished killing. The eyes unnerved me, and I nearly gasped again. I steadied myself, happy for her presence despite her worrisome gaze. I smiled as naturally as I could.

"Shite, Edweene. He was their master. It would have pleased me more if you had struck him down."

"I would have pursued but feared you to be engaged. I thought it better to come and ensure you still drew breath."

The knight drew his sword again and advanced toward Edweene. She glared at him and said, "I was unaware you had company, Aaron." She jumped lightly off the balcony and drew her curved sword. "Will I have to kill him too?"

"Stand down, Ser. This woman is my friend."

He halted his advance but did not remove his gaze from her. "You travel with strange friends, my lord. Something about her stinks of sacrilege."

"Maybe so," I said, unable to disagree wholly with the man. I moved to stand between them, intentionally keeping my back to her to demonstrate that I trusted her explicitly. "But, she is with me. If you make to fight her, you shall also cross steel with me."

He stared at me momentarily, his eyes filled with darkness—or something like it. Strange animosity came off of him in almost palpable waves. He breathed deeply and made the sign of the Star across his chest. "Very well," he said with a great, overblown show of trepidation, sighed loudly, and said, "I shall do as you wish."

"I wish for you to step back, Ser," I said, and he did.

"For now."

"What brings you here, Ser?" There would be plenty of time for dealing with other conflicts later, if there were a "later" for the three of us.

"*You* bring me here, my lord," he said, emphasizing the word, *You*.

"Not still pursuing me with stories aimed at turning me from my quest, are you?"

"You should listen, Aaron," Edweene's voice cut in. "I would hear his pitch. From what I understand of this night, you owe him that. You owe me that."

I did owe them both, I supposed, even if I was surprised that she would respond this way to a man who had just called her a sacrilege.

"Very well, Ser. Tell us your tale."

"As I said before, I would have you accompany me to free Ser Prenot. Nothing has changed." He gestured about the room with his arms wide. "Except this."

"Except this, indeed." I thought of the Gorgon warrior's words and innuendo about *secrets* and such. I thought of the note, the broken man on the Star: *All those that follow you shall perish, all those that assist you shall perish, and the knight, Prenot, shall die regardless.*

"Your mind works on something," Edweene said.

She knew me well, this lych. "Yes. My mind works on something." I turned to the knight. "Perhaps there is something to your request. I would know your name, Ser. You carry the sigil of Richeau. I would know why your heart is in this battle."

"My Lord," he said. He bowed slightly to me. "I am Dumont, son of Richeau, Earl of An Andor. At your service, Ser. Prenot is my brother, if truth be known. I would have his release."

Edweene whistled. "The reasons are clear now. There is no altruism buried beneath that glistening plate and five-pointed Star. It is but simple self-service."

Dumont made to draw his sword, but I held his hand. "You two must stop. I am sorry for your brother," I said. "There was a note stuck to the man on the Breaking Star—a note for me—which carried some cryptic references to Prenot. And the Gorgon also spoke of the knight's secrets here."

Interest sparked in Edweene's eyes—a flash of azure. I smiled at her unconsciously.

"I would read this note," Dumont said.

I fished it from my surcoat and passed it to him. He began to read it. Edweene sat upon the broken bed and began to sharpen her sword. In time, the knight handed the parchment back to me when he finished, his sharp eyes thoughtful. He clutched at the golden Star that hung about his neck and whispered something silently. I took it from him and handed it to Edweene. She unfolded it slowly and read. Her eyes narrowed as she did, their blueness sharp and bright. I stepped toward her, closer and hovered there, waiting for her to finish, my fingers fidgeting with my sword belt.

Impatient, I asked as she read it, "The man who escaped said he was the Tawl before he unleased the Gorgon. Do you know what—or who—the Tawl is?"

She took a moment to finish reading and then looked up, her eyes glittering in the candlelight. "It is a name that comes from Golish legends, myths of The Old Gods, really. In some myths, he's a legendary assassin, or warrior who stalks those who did not believe in the Old Gods. To the Temple of the Star, he is like the Devil on earth, or so I was taught when I was a Wife of The God. But, what I don't understand is that this message cited The God as well, as though the Tawl served not only The God, but the Old Gods also. It is a mystery."

"Could he be real? Could this Golish knight we saw tonight be the real Tawl?"

"He is a Devil. And he is real. The God—the bishop—warns of him," Ser Dumont said. He stepped away from us to stand on the balcony.

Leaning over, his gauntleted hands gripping the stone banister, he looked out at the dark courtyard below. He seemed to be nervous. He fidgeted his feet on the floor, stepping back and forth between them as he leaned. He whistle-hissed and turned around. His face was grim and dark, his hair was sweat-soaked and matted around his cheeks from his helmet. He narrowed his eyes. The flickering yellow candlelight made his face look otherworldly.

"Is this the same bishop you wish to discredit?" I asked. I tried to keep the sarcasm from my voice, but the irony was clear.

"Yes. That one. The bishop speaks the Covenant. The Covenant is not wrong. The Tawl is a heathen, at the very least, he is 'possessed of the Devil,' or his proxy in the Old Gods. We go to save Prenot, then," Dumont said. His voice was matter-of-fact, gritty. He stepped over the broken corpse of the Gorgon warrior and extended his hand to me.

I had no choice, or so it seemed. I looked from him to Edweene, scrutinizing the eyes of my two companions—one companion I'd known—if it could be described as such—for two years and more, and one who had just saved my life. We were going after the Tartans. We were going to get the young knight, Ser Prenot, and we were going to learn his secrets. If all went the way Dumont implied, Prenot would hold damning evidence against the bishop—or some other agent of The Temple—who'd sent him there in false service to The God.

I took Dumont's hand and shook it. It was a matter of convenience, and I felt hesitation in his grip. He didn't like me, and he liked Edweene even less. I squeezed hard and released, casting him an expression of defiance, smiling grimly.

"Do not take this mission of necessity as friendship," he said.

"I do not."

"You are a killer, Ser," said Dumont as he pulled his hand away. He rubbed it with his other as if he could scrub off the unclean. "I shall not forget that fact."

"Yet, here we are," Edweene's voice came from behind me. "All of your honor and all your right-eousness, Ser knight, and yet here you are, joining with a murderer and an apostate." Her voice twisted with a definite tone of wry satisfaction, even a small snicker—or perhaps I imagined that.

They were both right. I *was* a killer, and she *was* an apostate (which was the least of her sacrileges). I was still young and foolish; the Crusade was a way to find absolution from The God. I swore I would change. But, Edweene thought not, thought my nature set.

I have come to find that war is not glory and honor but death and terror and a living, breathing feeling of need that comes to exist inside. And the Archbishop's absolution? Well, that depends on your point of view. I planned on providing the bishop with the opportunity to find out for himself. If it meant I'd have to travel halfway across the Holy Land to free this foolish knight, then so be it.

Whenever I worked to find redemption, my dark skills seemed to draw me back to the ways I sought to subvert. Perhaps this was my destiny, my purpose for The God. If so, what did that mean for the Crusade, or honor?

At least this time, I sought to rescue and not to murder.

CHAPTER 6
A TWIST OF FATE

The next morning, I gazed outside from the Duveaux's balcony. We'd buried the bodies of Duveaux and his people last night—the ones we could find—and burned the dead of The Old Gods despite the protests by Dumont. It was their way, and I would not have them rotting in the sun. It was nearly morning, and I made ready to leave. We'd slept in the Duveaux's bedroom that night, buttoned up and ready for any attack that might come.

With God's providence, no attack came. My arms and shoulders were sore, and my leg, recently stitched up by Edweene, ached to the heavens. I heaved a sigh; despite the pain, it was time to go. My quest would not wait. I turned and strode from the room, down the stairs, and across the grounds to where we had stabled the horses.

Dumont was there. Edweene was not.

The gloaming was cool and wet. Rain hovered above the ground in a fog that soaked through surcoats and pads alike. The knight had prepared our two chargers and a pack horse, upon which he was still mounting the panniers—the pack harness where we would carry our stores of food and equipment for our quest. After a final check of our supplies and weapons, we mounted our horses and set off towards the Tartan territories, the rising sun at our backs.

Despite starting our trek on the road, the journey to come would be arduous, and the terrain would grow more treacherous with each passing mile. Soon, we would leave the Pilgrim's approach and head Southwest toward the ford across the River Rak, known as Dungorak, where we'd pass under the battlements of the fifth knuckle—Caer Gorak. Here, we would turn nearly due west and enter the land of the Gols. The fords were a hundred miles from where we were now, and the passing would be difficult through shrubs, wood, and rocky hills. We rode in silence, each lost in our own thoughts. The only sound was the steady rhythm of our horses' hooves against the old cobble road. As the sun reached its zenith, we stopped to rest in the shade of an oak thicket that grew close to the Approach, the boughs above providing a satisfying pool of shade—a welcome respite from the heat.

It was then that we heard approaching hoof-beats, the clatter of armor and weaponry unmistakable in the stillness.

"Quick, Ser . . ." I said and pulled my steed behind the trees. Dumont nodded and followed suit. I'd rather choose the way to face them, than be ridden down in the road, if I had my druthers. We drew our swords and crouched at the edge of the thicket. But as the rider drew closer, we recognized the colors of the Knights of the Holy Passage and the emblem of the order emblazoned upon the knight's surcoat. His helmet was strapped on his horse's flanks, and he was riding fast, his face hard and focused on the road ahead.

I didn't hesitate. I sheathed my sword, stepped out, and raised my arm in a signal. Dumont did likewise.

"Hoa . . . Ser knight," I called.

The rider reined in his steed some distance from us—far enough to allow for a charge if he so desired. His face was grim. The horse bounced and spun and settled, facing us.

"Announce yourself, Ser," he called.

I lowered my hand and remained steady, as unthreatening as I could manage, with my hand ready to draw steel. "Ser Aaron of Rivershire," and . . .

Dumont cut me off. "I am Dumont, son of Richeau, Earl of An Andor," he called out. "At your service, Ser."

The knight breathed a recognizable sigh of relief. He dismounted, his armor creaking as he approached us. "Ser Aaron, Ser Dumont," he said, his voice tight with urgency. "I bring grave news from The Stone." He hesitated a moment as emotion flashed across his young face.

"Speak, man," I said.

"Uh . . . yes," he said haltingly as if the words would strike him dead. "There has been an attempt on Commander Gavreaux's life, and the assassin has fled. I rode in pursuit and saw the bloody mess at the outpost. I fear they may be connected, and the villain may have allies in these lands."

A chill ran down my spine at the knight's words. I ignored the news of Duvreaux's estate, which we'd just left and was partially our doing. But who would dare to strike at Gavreaux within the walls of The Stone? "Tell me more," I said, my voice steady despite the unease that plagued my heart. "What happened, Ser knight, exactly?"

The knight shook his head, his eyes haunted. "It was a silent strike, My Lord. The assassin slipped into the knight Commander's chambers in the dead of night. Only by the grace of The God did he survive. His murderer was surprised by the chambermaid, by The grace of the Star. And the assassin managed to slip away, leaving the panic-stricken woman in tears and tatters. She screamed . . . as you can imagine. When the guards arrived, they found my lord bleeding out on his floor, deep gashes in his throat and chest—the result of a mad combat in the dark. He lives, but barely."

A wave of nausea washed over me. Gavreaux, a man to whom I owed so much, had come close to death. It was not lost on me that the assassin's methods, the silent attack, and the swift escape bore all the hallmarks of Edweene's deadly arts. And I knew she was there. But, did anyone else?

Dumont answered that question when he spoke next, his voice low and urgent. "Ser Aaron, I must tell you something."

I knew his words before he said them, and I cast him a glower.

He lowered his voice, speaking away from the Passage knight. "When I was at The Stone, I saw your dark friend, Edweene, there—I think. It was mere hours before the attack on Commander Gavreaux. She was in the shadows, watching, waiting. I fear she may have played some part in this treachery."

Perhaps it would not have bothered me if I hadn't entertained the same fears. But, as it was, the guilt, the anger at some potential betrayal, and my unwillingness to admit such a thing made my stomach turn and my eyes blaze with anger. I snapped self-righteously, "You'd dare accuse her? On what grounds? Edweene has been a true and loyal companion to me. I will not brook such baseless slander!"

Dumont stood his ground, his gaze unwavering. "It is not slander, Ser Aaron. I know what I saw. I don't know your friend, but she holds darkness in her. I can feel it."

"You do not know the lady, Ser," I said. "She has suffered much for The God."

That much was true—the suffering at the hands of The God. And Ser Dumont certainly did not know her. But I did. And she was more than capable of such an act. She also bore resentment against the Passage knights—though Dumont would know naught of that. I held on to the knowledge—or assumption—that if Edweene had tried to kill the Commander, he'd likely be dead. She did not leave many alive.

He responded, "Do her skills match those of the assassin? If so, you must consider the possibility that she is not what she seems."

I clenched my fists, fighting back the urge to strike him. Or cry out in despair. What about this woman—this lych—drove me so mad? I decided to change the discussion. I'd get to the bottom of this question—with her! Ser Dumont had naught to do with it. "And what of our mission? We need the lady, and her weapons on this trek. We will need to infiltrate whatever Gol fortress holds our wayward knight. Your fighting skills are fine, but you haven't the stealth required for some of what awaits. Would you have me abandon this mission on the suggestions of guilt from a man who has no evidence and has shown nothing but disdain for Edweene from the start?"

The Passage knight stepped between us; his hands raised in a placating gesture. "Peace, Sers. This bickering will get us nowhere. Ser Aaron, I understand your loyalty to your companion. Still, if the Lady Edweene, whomever that is, was indeed in the Stone and has the skills and predisposition to do such a Godless thing, then Ser Dumont's concerns are not without merit. We must investigate this matter thoroughly for Commander Gavreaux's sake and the Holy Land's safety—and, of course, for our honor to remain intact."

I took a deep breath, forcing myself to calm down. The knight was wise, of course, and my will was filled with sin. Honor be damned. I could not bring myself to admit that Edweene would ever come under my sword again. But I also could not let my personal feelings cloud my judgment.

"Very well," I said, my voice tight. "I will aid you in your search for the assassin. Commander Gavreaux is an honorable knight, and I cannot stand idly by while his life is in danger. But I must also see my mission through—a mission with even more gravity than this and one of which you have no knowledge. Whatever the case with Edweene and the murderer, it cannot wait."

The Passage knight nodded, eyes hard and disapproving. "I understand, Ser Aaron. I will not ask you to abandon your quest. But if you should find any sign of the assassin in your travels, send word to The Stone. Commander Gavreaux's life may depend on it."

"Agreed," I said, added, "When you arrive in Clurak, Ser, you must inform the king of the raid on the outpost and the taking of Deveaux. The king's men and the Orders should increase patrols. Bands of Gols are within the Holy Land, killing the faithful."

"I shall. You know, my lord, it is the sacred duty of the Passage knights to secure this road. And we shall do just that. But first, I must ride and seek out this assassin and inform the king—and the bishop—of the attempt on his most humble servant's life. We shall find those that perpetrated this evil, and—"

I interrupted him, wishing to avoid the admonition of Duty to The God and his people. "And Ser, please take word to my captain, Ser Wilhem. He is under my banner in the Crusader camp outside Clurak, of the same."

"Yes, my lord," he added, a bit nonplussed at my rudeness.

"Well, enough, Ser. My gratitude to you,"

He nodded. "Best be gone, Ser," he added. "The sun does not wait."

With that, the knight mounted and galloped off, his armor glinting in the sun and the star on his tunic, a blood-red mark against the landscape, until at last he disappeared into the distance. Dumont and I exchanged a long look, the weight of our new burden settling upon our shoulders. I liked the man but couldn't shake the feeling that our lives were bound to come into deadly conflict. If it came to it, would I choose him or Edweene? That answer was simple, and I knew I had no choice, Honor or Duty aside. There was something with Edweene that made me mad. Edweene was me, I knew. In so many ways, she had made me. I finally looked away from him. "Let's get gone, Ser," I said.

I don't know if he nodded or whispered his agreement, but I heard his saddle creak. I took that to mean he was ready. I stretched my back and spurred my mount on, but as I did, a flash of movement caught my eye. That blasted raven was perched on a nearby tree branch. Its blue eyes seemed to bore into me as if it could sense the turmoil within my heart.

"That bird," Dumont said, his voice low and wary. "I've seen you watching it. It has been following us since Duveaux's. I mislike the look of it."

I shook my head and turned away from the raven. "It is just a bird, Dumont," I lied. "A strange one, perhaps, but nothing more. We have more pressing matters to attend to."

Dumont looked unconvinced but said nothing more as we gathered up the pack horse and rode on. The raven took flight, its black wings cutting through the air as it soared ahead of us, as if leading the way.

As we rode, my thoughts were a maelstrom of doubt and suspicion. Could Edweene truly have betrayed us? And if so, why? What dark purpose drove her actions? I thought of the times she had saved my life and the times I'd saved hers. I thought of all the dangerous and deep secrets we shared. I thought of those eyes when I'd driven my blade through her and how they still haunt me. She had been a constant presence in my life for so long, a guiding light in the darkness of the Crusades. The idea that she could be a traitor was almost too much to bear.

Yet, I could not deny the evidence before me: the assassin's methods, Dumont's account of seeing her at The Stone. It all pointed to a terrible truth I did not want to face. I knew only one thing for certain: the road ahead would be fraught with danger, and the price of failure would be higher than ever before. I had to find the truth, no matter the cost, for the sake of Gavreaux, the innocent lives at stake, and my own twisted and sin-corrupted soul.

As the sun began to set, we made camp in a small clearing, to the side of the Approach Road. Tomorrow, we'd leave the road and head toward the Fords. The raven perched on a nearby tree branch, its eyes glinting in the fading light. Watching. Always watching. I sat by the fire, sharpening my blade and trying to quiet the storm of emotions that tormented me.

Dumont sat across from me, his gaze fixed on the dancing flames. He seemed to hesitate a moment before interrupting my reverie. "Aaron," he said, his voice low and serious. "I know you care for the woman, but you must be prepared for the possibility that she is not what she seems. If she is truly behind the attack on Commander Gavreaux, we will have no choice but to do our Duty."

I met his gaze, my eyes hard and unyielding. "I will do what I must, Dumont. I have faced more than my share of hardship . . . and tragedy." I thought deeply about the next words, letting the silence of the night fill me with its calmness. Then I added, "But I will not condemn her until we have proof of her guilt. She deserves the benefit of the doubt, at least from me."

Dumont nodded, his expression grim. "As you say, Ser. But do not let your feelings blind you to the truth. We have a Duty to fulfill, and we cannot let personal attachments stand in the way of that."

I said nothing, my gaze returned to the fire. Dumont was right, of course. But the thought of Edweene being a traitor, of having to face her as an enemy once again, like all those years ago . . . it was almost too much to bear.

As I lay down to rest that night, my mind was filled with dark thoughts and troubling dreams. The raven watched over me, its blue eyes glinting in the moonlight, a silent sentinel in the darkness. I wasn't sure whether to feel comfort from that, or discomfited.

CHAPTER 7
A RIFT AND A REVELATION

The morning sun crept over the horizon, night still held the land in grayness and a hint of a glow spread out from The God's twilight when Edweene returned to us. Dumont and I were packing our gear, preparing to continue the journey. I unintentionally separated from Dumont as I packed the panniers on the far side of the pack horse when she emerged from the shadows like a wraith. "Aaron," she hissed and startled me.

I spun to face her, hand at my hilt.

"I could have slit your throat, Ser knight," she teased, her eyes sparkling. "So soon you forget the ways of the Dark Man," she remarked.

As she stepped through the brush, I felt a mixture of relief and apprehension. The accusations Dumont had leveled against her the day before still weighed heavily on my mind, and I knew I could not let them go unaddressed.

I found my voice. "Edweene," I said, trying my best to ignore the conflicted feelings of joy at seeing her and despair at what it could mean. I kept my voice low and serious. "We need to talk, my lady."

Her blue eyes glinted in the dim light as she met my gaze, and for a moment, I was transported back to that night when we first battled, the night that started this unholy connection. The last night of her life, when I'd looked into those very eyes, and she'd begged me to take her home—I knew what she'd meant, she'd begged me to kill her. And I did. I slipped my knife between her ribs and watched the life slip from those same eyes. It has haunted me ever since.

"My lady?" she asked, laughed under her breath for an awkward moment, and then became serious. "I know, Aaron. And I'm ready to explain what I can of it, anyway."

Dumont stepped forward, his hand resting on the hilt of his sword. "I would hear this . . . explanation," he muttered, his tone dripping with sarcasm.

For my part, I had not realized that he was listening in, and I shot him a warning look before turning back to Edweene. "Ser Dumont here," I motioned my thumb over my shoulder at Dumont, believes he saw you at The Stone mere hours before the attempt on Commander Gavreaux's life. I can't speak to that." I let the lie from my lips so easily. I knew she was there, of course. I met with her in my apartment. But I wanted to give her a chance to speak her peace or fabricate an excuse to give to Dumont. I continued, "If so, what were you doing there, Edweene?"

Edweene knows me as well as I know myself. She sighed, her shoulders slumping slightly. "I was there to gather information, Aaron. About the Passage knights, their movements, and their plans. I . . . I have a history with them. You know this more than anyone. How could you think I would let sleeping dogs remain asleep?"

I felt a surge of anger and betrayal at her words: I'd given her a chance at least to lay the ground-work for a life-saving lie, but she'd taken the way of truth. It burned in me—perhaps it was some conviction that she'd been more virtuous than I, that she'd allowed me to lie for her—sacrifice my own honor, and that she'd reserved that for her-self—at least in this moment, on this road, with these circumstances. "You lied to me, Edweene? The connection between us is no small thing. We've always . . ." I shook my head. I couldn't continue with that line of thought . . . "And yet, you've been keeping secrets from me all this time? Why would you not tell me?"

She shook her head, her expression pained, eyes soft and apologetic. "I didn't lie, Aaron. I just . . . I didn't want you to be implicated in my vendetta. I sought only to protect you, my lord. The Passage Knights—and that bastard

Gavreaux left me, man. I saw it in his eyes. He smiled as I went down. Mocked me at my last—"

I remember wondering at the time why they'd left her. Why she'd not come home, but, I'd justified it. I saw her go under in that melee. I figured the knights had, too. "Edweene, what—"

"Stop Aaron. You could not see in the melee. The escape was mad. But I did. That man—Gavreaux—looked me dead in the eyes and smiled that self-righteous—never mind Aaron, you'll not believe . . . or understand how others see me because you see me that way too, even if you deny it. I may be dead, but I'm not without value or without feeling. My heart may not beat as yours, but it is as full of life as yours. You at least sense that. Others . . ." the woman shot a look toward Dumont, who now was standing, arms folded over the back of the packhorse, chin in hands, watching. ". . . Others do not."

"Lady Edweene," I started with her honorific, and she waved me to be quiet.

"No, Aaron. I'll have my revenge, and not because he left me for dead, but because he did it to kill me—an abomination—and send me to the hell he thinks I belong in, despite having helped kill an enemy of the Crusade. I am a stain on him. On you, hero of the Crusade. But I never meant for it to interfere with your mission or put you in danger. By exposing the bishop, we are united."

Dumont scoffed, his eyes narrowing, confused and judging. I wondered if he understood Edweene's references to her death, her non-beating heart. He said flatly, "This is a likely story. How do we know you're not giving voice to what we both know are Ser Aaron's desires? For all we know, you could be working with the Tawl, trying to sabotage our efforts from within. And none of this excuses murder. My lord, Aaron, honor dictates we—"

I held up my hand, silencing Dumont's accusations. "Enough. We don't have time for this. We must keep moving and stay ahead of the Tawl and his forces. We shall save honor's dictums for another day."

Dumont scoffed. "Well enough, my lord, but we'll face that decision soon enough—"

"So be it," I said to him. "We'll face it when we must." I turned to Edweene, my expression grave.

"I want to believe you, Edweene. But you must understand how this looks. If you're keeping secrets from me, how can I trust you?"

Edweene met my gaze, her eyes shining with fierce determination. "I have always been loyal to you, Aaron." She went silent for a moment and seemed to contemplate something. Then she added, "Since the day you saved me with your dagger to my heart. You remember it?" My eyes welled with shame-filled tears. I resisted wiping them away. A knight. A Dark Man does not shed tears. Regardless, she didn't wait for me to answer before going on. "I'll prove my loyalty to you, Aaron. I will show you my heart is true."

I nodded, feeling a weight settle in my chest. "Edweene, you don't—"

"Yes, Aaron . . . I would have your back. Something has changed in you. I see you look at me, and—"

"Ser," Dumont interrupted us. "We'd best go. This is all so very touching, but we've got a knight to save. Remember him?"

We remained silent. We quickly broke camp, packing up our gear and saddling our horses.

Tension was high between Edweene and Dumont, and the air was thick with unspoken accusations and barely contained hostility. And me?
I was worried. What was in the Lady Edweene's
mind? What were her true motivations? She'd always been the better person than me, but things
were getting confusing. My singular mission—to
expose the bishop's traitorous acts—was now all
twisted up with vendettas, rescues, and divided
loyalties.

As we rode out, we left the main road and
headed towards the Fords—a straight ride, no
matter how rough the terrain—into Golish territory. A desire for speed drove us and to avoid un-
wanted attention from the Tawl's scouts or spies.
It was not long before the terrain grew rougher
as we left the well-traveled path, and the ground
became rocky and uneven beneath our horses'
hooves. We rode in silence.

Two hours later, we guided our horses through
a small draw between two rocky hills. The ground
was rough, and the horses were having a hard
time with it. I remembered my old steed Sway-
back from all those years ago. He was a good

steed and sturdy. This animal was stronger and faster but lacked my old mount's reliability, requiring all my focus to manage him.

I was so focused on the ground underfoot that four riders emerged from the ragged, low trees a hundred feet ahead and charged headlong toward us. They wore chain armor and did not have any device or sigil that would tell me who they were. Glinting in the sunlight, their curved scimitars and barbed spears told me they were likely Gols. Despite the rough ground, they rode with frightening speed.

I drew my blade, preparing to attack when Edweene sped past me, her own horse lighter and swifter than mine, plunging into the thick brush. She must have been aware of them, keeping her eyes alert as I tried to manage the trail at the head of our tiny column. Whatever the case, the Nun was well into the attack, just as I was getting ready to respond.

Behind me, Dumont pushed slowly ahead, too, his horse coming alongside mine. He hesitated for the slightest moment and looked sidelong at me. I ignored the man's looks and spurred my mount. "The enemy is up there, man!"

Combat moves quickly, perceptions slow down, and senses are heightened. It seems like hours, but the small fights are over in seconds. Too much longer, and Edweene would be alone among the four killers. And indeed, Edweene was off her horse and spinning up beside the lead attacker, narrowly avoiding his leveled spear as he sallied past her in the rush.

The second horseman pulled up and raised his spear to throw down on her just as Edweene slid her sword along the tendons in the lead horse's foreleg, sending it screaming into the hard ground and propelling the lead rider over the horse's head to slam into the ground in front of me.

The second rider released the spear, but Edweene was too quick and deflected it away with her sword. And then he drew his sword, and the third rider was bearing down on her from behind with his curved saber held out for a textbook cavalry thrust.

I couldn't focus for long, as I had my own to worry about. The lead rider was good. He hit the ground hard, rolled, and came up, perhaps a bit stunned but in a ready position, drawing his blade as he did. When I was in range, I slashed down on him, my blade sliding along his and hammering into this crosspiece. The force of my blow drove him back, and I pressed my advantage, pushing my horse into him, and dividing him from the larger melee. As he recovered from the force of my blow, he tried to spin away, but I sliced, in short, quick slashes. My attacks outclassed his awkward attempts to parry and hit him high on the shoulder. The blade slid off his mail, deflecting up and into the side of his throat, halted by the coif there. But he fell back, dropped his weapon, and grasped at the ineffectual strike, clearly worried that I'd struck a mortal blow. His hesitation cost him, and I drove forward, leaning over my mount's withers and sliding my sword into the man's open-faced helm. He fell immediately as the point of my weapon penetrated the softness of his eye sockets and nose bridge.

I spun my horse, expecting to see Dumont fighting alongside Edweene. But to my shock and horror, I saw him holding back, his sword drawn but motionless, as he watched two warriors bear down on her.

"The God damn you, man," I cried and rushed ahead as a scimitar deflected off Edweene's leather jerkin. She returned a thrust up into his ribcage, sending him sprawling backward from his horse.

It should have been her last move, as the horseman behind her raised to cleave her from behind. She was rotating to meet him and raising her weapon in a vain attempt to parry, but it was too late. I panicked. My heart leaped into my throat as I watched in that strange, slow motion that comes in combat, the object of so much of my pain and desire and hate and torment dancing her beautiful death ballet for perhaps the last time. I was too far away and out of position to intervene. Out of sheer desperation, I flung my sword at the man.

It paid off. The weapon did no damage, but it banged him in the shoulders threw him off balance, and confused him. His downward slash went wide, and he instinctively looked toward me, taking his attention away from the more dangerous threat below him. It took seconds for the lych to spin, slash him across his thigh, and, as he cried out and bent over, tear her blade across his throat—this one had no mail coif—sending him backward, out of his saddle and into the stony ground with a loud thump.

Just then, Dumont arrived at the melee. But it was over. He was too late.

As I leaped off the horse to ensure the man never got up again, driving my dagger into him, a singular figure emerged from the trees where they had attacked. I recognized the helmet that ended below his eyes and the A mail veil below it. I recognized the steel brigandine and the long falchion, all despite the black cloak billowing like a shadow behind him. It was the Tawl.

He met my gaze momentarily, before turning and disappearing back into the forest. I made to pursue him, but Edweene's cry of pain stopped me in my tracks. I turned to see her kneeling on the ground, her hand pressed to a deep gash on her side. Apparently the armor had not completely stopped the Gol's blade.

Dumont stood over her, his expression unreadable.

"Edweene!" I cried, rushing to her side. "What happened?"

She looked up at me, her eyes narrowed and blazing with anger and betrayal. "Dumont . . . is either useless or a coward," she spoke plainly. "He left me to die here . . ."

I turned to Dumont, my hand tightening on the hilt of my sword. "Dumont?"

Dumont met my gaze, his expression cool and unrepentant. "I did what I had to do, Aaron. I had to watch the rear; in case we were set upon from behind. You know the Gol's are wont to do such. Besides, she handled herself well."

I shook my head, feeling a wave of disgust wash over me. "By The God, Dumont."

The knight made the sign of the Star as I took The God's name in vain, the hypocritical action angering me even more. Dumont is not a coward; I'd seen the man fight. He was more than competent with a blade, perhaps my equal in man-to-man combat. Then that could mean . . .

"Dumont, Edweene is one of us . . . if you can't see that, perhaps it's you we can't trust."

"Perhaps, Ser, but do not question my honor. I told you why I hung back, and it is the truth. Look in your heart, and you will know. If I had abandoned the rear, and the Gol had done as they usually do, then we would all be dead now. You know this to be true."

Edweene struggled to her feet. She still pressed her hand to her wounded side. She turned to face me, her expression fierce and determined. "I'm going after the Tawl, Aaron."

"You cannot," I said. "You are wounded, my lady. He will surely kill you."

"Do you forget who I am, Aaron? What I am? The cut will heal. And . . . I will show you where my loyalties lie."

I reached out to her, my heart heavy with worry and fear. "Edweene, no. It's too dangerous. We need to stay together, now more than ever." As I said it, I felt to the worry of having her and

Dumont together, and the pang of betrayal about
the Gavreaux matter.

My unease must have been in my eyes. For, she
shook her head and frowned. "I'm sorry, Aaron.
But this I will do. There is no stopping this. I will
return to you, I swear it. As I always do. But first
. . . I must face the Tawl. Perhaps I can keep him
from interfering with your Rescue."

With that, she turned, went to her horse and
took its reins, then limped off into the forest, her
sword clutched tightly in her hand.

I watched her go, feeling a hollow ache in my
chest. Dumont stood beside me. His presence
was not comforting.

"She's abandoning us, my lord," he said, his
voice low and serious. "As I said she would. We
can't trust her, Ser. I do not know what you feel.
I cannot say. But The God is not with that one. I
think you know this."

But even as he spoke the words, I couldn't
shake the feeling that there was more to this than
met the eye. Edweene had saved me, more than
once. And in more ways than just physical. I had
murdered her once, as she'd asked. And when it

came to it, she'd repaid me. Over and again. It was because of Edweene that I knew the bishop was corrupted. Because of her, I understood the contradictions in the Crusade. This war was just . . . and it also wasn't just. And she made me better. The God would know this. The God had to know this.

I would do my best to stop this mad vendetta against The Passage Knights, but I would not abandon her. If it came to a decision between her and Gavreaux . . . well, I just hoped it wouldn't.

I turned to Dumont, my expression grave and my voice firm. "We continue on our mission, Dumont. But we do not abandon Lady Edweene." I avoided doing what I wanted right then, which was to drive my dagger into the man. After all, he was only a man, sword to the Crusade, just like me. And he had the same proclivities and foibles as I did. I'd not kill him for that. But I'd also rather not stoke the flames. I knew he was wrong about her—I hoped it anyway. I finished my statement, "We will need her before the end."

Dumont looked like he wanted to argue, but something in my expression must have convinced him otherwise. He nodded, his jaw tight and his eyes hard.

"As you say, my lord. But mark my words . . . this will not end well for any of us."

"Your words are duly marked, Ser," I said, ending it. I fixed my gaze on the spot where Edweene had disappeared into the trees. It would get harder from here. But, if I knew Edweene, she would not rest until she was by my side once more. As much as she thought she had to prove something, I felt the same.

Our fates were intertwined, for better or for worse.

CHAPTER 8

THE FORD OF DUNGORAK

We went on another few miles to get out of the area—the dead tend to attract all manner of nasty creatures in this part of the world—before we stopped and made our camp. We went mostly in silence, my anger with Dumont amplified by the oppressive atmosphere endemic to this broken land. It was bad enough here in the Holy Land, but soon, we would travel into the Gols' lands. It was bound to get worse.

I pushed that thought away as we found a spot, secluded and in the heavy brush, away from any obvious animal or creature trails. I wanted no one to find us. I needed to rest and think. Already, the Tawl knew we were coming. There had always been no question in my mind that he was probably keeping eyes on us since we left Duveaux's estate. But it was still unnerving to know we were being stalked and watched. I preferred to be the one stalking. Perhaps it was my days in the Dark Men when I'd abandoned the stupidity of honorable combat for the much more palatable concept of fighting with little regard for such things.

Of course, it was a double-edged sword. When I'd done so, I'd lost myself. But Edweene had found me and helped me find myself in a most peculiar and heart-wrenching way. And now, I was walking a strange line. I was rescuing a fool from certain death—something that should be honorable, yet I could not help feeling there was something more to it. Could Ser Prenot and his cohort have accidentally entered the Gol Land? It's nigh impossible. That could only mean that they were put up to it, and if Dumont was to be believed, there was a connection between that so-called mistake and the bishop's betrayal of The God and The Temple. These were the thoughts plaguing me when, at last, I fell off to sleep, my head resting on my saddle harness, and my riding cloak pulled tight around me.

The next morning, I woke to a heavy heart and a mind still clouded with doubt. As I prepared for the day's journey, my thoughts were consumed by the previous day's events. Edweene's admission of her vendetta against the Passage Knights, Dumont's hesitation during the battle, and the Tawl's ominous appearance swirled in my mind, forming a tangled web of uncertainty.

I glanced at Dumont, who was already packing his bedroll and makeshift camp. The knight's movements were precise and efficient, as always, but there was a tension in his shoulders that hadn't been there before. He seemed preoccupied. Our eyes met momentarily, and I saw a flicker of something in his gaze—suspicion, perhaps, or even a hint of guilt. I doubted the latter.

Dumont had fought well at Duveaux's, but I could not shake the feeling that he was hiding something. I certainly believed him when he said he wished to rescue his brother, but there was something more there. Something more sinister, or perhaps self-serving, than that.; He'd hardly talked of his kin since we left, which left me questioning what that relationship was, and what his true motives were, if it was not to as was presented.

I shook my head, trying to clear my thoughts. I couldn't afford to be distracted, not now. We had a mission to complete, and every moment we delayed was another moment that Prenot remained in enemy hands.

As we mounted our horses and set off, I couldn't help but feel a pang of longing for Edweene's presence. Despite the secrets and the doubts, she had been a constant companion, a source of strength and guidance in the chaos of the Crusade. Without her, the road ahead seemed longer and more treacherous than ever before.

We rode in silence for a time; the only sound was the steady clopping of our horses' hooves against the rocky ground. The terrain, already difficult, grew more hostile with each passing mile, rugged ground giving way to jagged rocks and deep cuts in rocky hills. I kept my eyes moving from the ground before me to scan ahead for any signs of trouble to our flanks and the high ground around us. I had no desire to fall into an ambush like yesterday. It wasn't lost on me that, had the Gols been archers or worse, sorcerers, we might have been killed.

I felt naked without Edweene and unconsciously checked on my chivalric companion now and again. But he always nodded back when our eyes met, preoccupied as he was with watching for ambushers.

Of course, the raven was nowhere to be seen. Since we left Duveaux's estate, the bird had been a constant presence, watching over us with those eerie blue eyes. The skies were empty now, which was more disconcerting than it should have been. I knew when Edweene left, so too would the bird, but half—or more—of me had wished it was only a threat, and she was tailing us, watching out for us from the shadows or brush—a fool's notion.

As the sun climbed higher in the sky, we saw signs of the enemy's presence—or signs of Crusader patrols from the Knuckles. It was hard to tell, moving as fast as we were. Abandoned

campsites, discarded gear, weapons, animal carcasses—all these things pointed to the fact that
we were drawing closer to Golish territory. My
hand never strayed far from my sword hilt, and
I could see Dumont's posture mirroring mine.

We had been riding for hours when we finally
reached the River Rak—a wide, rushing torrent
that split the Holy Land in two. Many times, the
river had limited the advance of Golish forces
from the west as they pushed in from their natural homelands there. But the Gols now controlled
the land south of the knuckles for a hundred
years. Now, to the Crusaders, the river was a
strategic lifeline for many of the forts, bringing
logistics and support to be offloaded at Dungorak and ferried overland by wagon and porter
to the gates of the Crusader fort at Caer Gorak,
whose battlements overlooked the very fords we
were about to cross. The river served the same
purpose for the Gols—but from the other direction—ferrying supplies down from their moun-
tain forts deep in the Rak Mountains and the
Devil's Forest. More than once, Golish engineers

had tried to dam the waters or divert them. But the waters were too powerful, too deep.

Today, the river was swollen from recent rains high in the Rak Mountains to the south and west. Crossing it would be no easy feat, particularly because we desired secrecy. The Crusader garrison in the Caer could not be allowed to see us. This was an unsanctioned mission—and one which had the propensity to re-ignite open hostilities between the Crusade and the Gols—at least here along the frontier. Perhaps the king finding the bodies at Duveaux's estate would have the same or worse implications once the Passage Knight we spoke to told of it. However, the Crusade didn't have the strength to start an open war. I doubted the king would push things that far. The Gols, on the other hand, were an entirely different matter. Disavowing these raids would only go so far, especially if the Crusade persisted and struck deep into Golish territories. The Gols had very few inhibitions, like the Crusade. And they had the numbers, by The God.

We were crouched among boulders and brush on a small hill looking toward Caer Gorak; our horses hobbled some distance behind us in a low spot beneath the hill. The fort and the rushing waters of Dungorak were a quarter mile distant. It was late afternoon, and the sun was beginning to wane, sliding toward the western horizon and illuminating the blocky central keep of the fort like a black obelisk. On the walls and towers, the sentries were beginning to light the oil lanterns, and the gate was closed and the bridge drawn up.

Here, the deep waters of the Rak shallowed—though I suppose shallow is the wrong term. The river remained deep, but some ancient construction was built a mere four or five feet beneath the water line—and less so when the river did not run deep. Who built the structure and when, no one can remember. A series of tunnels under the broad, flat stone platform allowed the river to flow freely beneath and through. Perhaps once, it was a bridge of sorts, I remember wondering. Regardless, the structure prevents riverine travel up and down the Rak beyond this point. And it provides a useful—and strategic—area over which one can move without the use of a ferry or bridge—something we intended to do.

I glanced at Dumont, who was surveying the riverbank with a critical eye.

"The Tawl could not cross here. The tower is too vigilant," he said. "Which means he is still with us . . . here . . . somewhere." He rotated his head around as if he could possibly see our enemy.

"Do not be so sure, Ser," I said.

"But, how, then?" he asked, his tone implying me to be some ignoramus.

But I had seen more than most. I'd fought in the Crusade for more years than any I knew. And I'd survived by being smart, not strong—and not assuming anything. "There are ways, Dumont."

"Ways? A hidden ford, we are not aware of? A bridge or ferry?"

"No, Ser. Of course not. Such would be common knowledge. Cannot be hidden for long. Other ways. Ways you and I would not—or, could not—partake of."

"Sorcery," he exclaimed, and his voice lowered. He narrowed his eyes and peered around as though some dark force might hear him speak of it. I nearly laughed.

"Yes, Ser. Sorcery."

"Unfortunately, we have no such powers. We'll have to ford it," he said grimly. "There's no other way across."

I nodded, steeling myself for the task ahead. The whole point of coming here was that it was the only way across, other than the bridge on the Approach Road we'd chosen to avoid. Yes, we had to ford. But we had to do it quietly—and we'd have to wait until nightfall.

When it became dark, we let the night darken a bit longer, hopeful that the sentries would become tired or complacent, before we led our horses around the low hill to the water's edge. There was no official road on this side of the river, as trade and provisioning off loaded on the Caer's bank. But the ground was well worn, and the route well used—at least relative to the wilderness around. A path followed the eastern side of the river both north and south, dipping in and out of the brush as it followed the bank.

We led our horses to the water's edge, doing our best to maintain silence. I was well versed in the ways of the assassin and found myself confounded by Dumont's squeaking armor and stumbling gait. This is not to say he was not dexterous. He was a warrior, trained to fight and kill, not to skulk. His skills lay elsewhere. But still, it seemed silent enough. I squatted at the bank and waited, fiddling with my steed's rein in my hand.

"Ser . . . what—" he began to asked.

I looked him in the eye and pressed my finger to my lips, signaling him to silence. I whispered. "Quiet, Ser. Let us wait and listen. Let us make sure it is safe to cross."

He nodded and crouched near me. Our horses shifted nervously and silently. It seemed they were as on edge as I was. The landscape was unnaturally silent. On the walls, I could see the guards' silhouettes as they walked to and from between the merlons atop the palisade. We sat there for long minutes, which seemed to me to be hours, until I was satisfied that none were about, or if they were, they were working hard not to be seen or heard.

I signaled Dumont forward while I stood and led my horse into the water. The current was swift here, tugging at our legs as we waded in.

It seemed icy cold, and a bit of a shiver ran the length of my back. Beside me, Dumont gritted his teeth, his face a mask of concentration.

Halfway across the river, fate made its presence known, and disaster struck. Dumont suddenly stumbled and crashed into the water. The current dragged him under. For a moment, he fought his way back to his feet, and he thrust himself unsteadily up, gasping for air. But, the weight of his armor, or some loose stone, or other unfortunate thing conspired against him, and he stumbled and went back under. His hand grasped at me, and I lashed out taking it in mine, hauling him back to his feet.

Dumont's face was a mask of embarrassment in the near-dark, and I suppressed a desire to laugh at him. But the sound of the struggle seemed to echo through the silence, and my fear of discovery overcame my mirth. "Hurry, now," I hissed at him. "We must move quickly now."

He nodded, and we forged on, struggling through the rest of the crossing, our horses pulled behind on tethers. As we emerged on the other side of the river, I turned to Dumont, my breath coming in ragged gasps.

"Are you well, Ser?" I asked as quietly as I could.

"Yes. Thank you," he said, his voice hoarse, just a whisper. "For a moment, I feared that current would drag me away." He smiled at me and shook his head. "I feel a fool."

"No, Ser. The current is swift there—" I began to respond when the sound of war cries split the air.

My heart jumped into my throat, and my breath caught. I spun toward the sound in the direction of the fort, drawing my sword as I did. Dumont followed suit. Not twenty paces from us, a group of armored men—twenty, if there was one—wearing the sign of the Star stood and leered at us. At the front of them was a man I knew well: Geoffroi de Lyanha, the Lord of Dungorak.

He smiled like a cat and said, "I've been expecting you, my Lord Aaron of Rivershire. It has been a long, long time."

CHAPTER 9
CAER GORAK

The fortress of Caer Gorak loomed before us, its dark stone walls an imposing black against the darkening night sky. Geoffroi de Lyanha led the way, his men flanking us on either side as we crossed the drawbridge and passed through the iron gates.

"You must have left before the sun fell," I told my escort. "We had been watching the gate since midday."

"Aaron, Ser . . . you have forgotten much since your days in the Dark," Geoffroi responded back. He seemed happy to have captured me, which made some sense, given our history. When Ser Geoffroi spoke of the Dark, he referred to my days as a Dark Man, the assassin who worked for the Temple of the Star. Crusaders without honor. Despised, feared, and respected by the knights and men on both sides. We had served together in the Crusade before I went to the Dark, something he had disapproved of at the time.

"Ah..." I spoke and nodded. "There is another way."

"As you know, there is always another way."

We crossed the fortified bailey and pushed open the iron-bound doors into the central fortress, where we passed through the second palisade and into another, smaller, internal field. It was laid out in an organized militaristic fashion, with weapons racks, sparring dummies, and archery targets. Everything was quiet and eerie this late, the dummies looking from the black like ghostly figures. We passed them, our boots shuffling in the gravel and echoing on the walls. At some point, a livery boy took our mounts. We gave them without complaint—it would have been futile anyway. Soon, we pushed open the reinforced doors of the central keep.

As large as the fortress seemed on the outside, the inside was simple and utilitarian, even confined. It was built for warfare, logistics, and little else. Inside the central keep, it was no different than the outer bailey and the barbican. The lord of the keep was a soldier and always had been—at least since my days in the Crusade. Once, there had been a village surrounding the fort, but it had long since been removed—though removed may not be the best term. It had suffered so much from incursions, raids, and sieges that it had ceased to exist; the peasants and farmers that once tried to make a go of it fled north to safer territories. Nothing of it remained. And so it was much more important to keep the river open—it was the sole source of supplies for the castle. Caer Gorak was now a hard point, a Knuckle, in the Crusade's fist. Its role: to keep the Gols from controlling the River Rak north of the fords. It performed this task most effectively, to my recollection.

As we navigated the cold, stone corridors, I felt eyes on me and thought I'd caught a glimpse of a fleeting shadow dashing from one pool of shadow to another. I dismissed it as paranoia caused by the austere atmosphere permeating

every inch of the castle. The walls were bare, save
for the occasional torch flickering in its sconce,
casting long shadows across the cold stone. A
sense of unease settled in the pit of my stomach,
a feeling that only intensified as we proceeded
into the heart of the fortress. To my surprise,
Dumont and I were not bound or shackled as
we walked. The absence of chains was a small
comfort, but it did little to ease the tension in
the air. I glanced at Dumont, trying to gauge his
reaction, but his expression was inscrutable, his
eyes fixed straight ahead.

Geoffroi led us to a small, windowless room
within the castle keep. It was sparsely furnished,
with only a few wooden chairs and a large table
dominating the center of the space. Upon the
table, a detailed map was spread out, depicting
the Holy Land, the Rak Mountains, and the Devil's Forest in intricate detail. The sight of it sent
a chill down my spine, a reminder of the dangers
that lay ahead . . . and dangers I'd faced in years
past when I campaigned after the Archbishop
first called the Crusade all those years ago.

"Please, sit," Geoffroi said, gesturing to the chairs. His tone was cordial, almost friendly. But I knew Geoffroi well, and an undercurrent of tension in his voice set my nerves on edge.

I took my seat and noticed a flicker of movement in the corner of my eye. Turning my head, I saw a black cat in the corner of the room, deep in the shadows, its unnerving blue eyes fixed upon me. The sight of the animal was both disconcerting and strangely comforting. I felt that familiar tug that came when Edweene was nearby, and I wondered what it meant.

Geoffroi cleared his throat, returning my attention to the matter. "I must admit, I was surprised to receive word of your coming," he said, his eyes flicking between Dumont and me. "I am told of a secret mission sanctioned by the king himself, yet I was not informed of the details."

"A secret mission?" I asked. What madness was afoot? "I'm afraid I don't understand, my lord."

Geoffroi leaned forward, his elbows resting on the table. "A message delivered by a raven, bearing the seal of the Passage Knights. It spoke of your mission, of the importance of aiding you in your quest."

Beside me, Dumont shifted in his seat. His mouth was closed tight. After some time, he said, "And what, exactly, did this message say?" The man's voice was low and dripped with suspicion.

Geoffroi shook his head. "I'm afraid you would know more than I. The note was clear. I am not to ask Ser Aaron about his mission. I am to provide you what help I can. This is quite unconventional, Ser. Orders from the Knight Commander—on behalf of the King? I have no precedent in this."

I felt a surge of frustration at his words. The King had not sanctioned this mission, and the involvement of the Passage Knights only deepened the mystery. "I don't understand," I said, my voice rising in spite of myself. "Why would the Passage Knights send a message about our mission, and why would they keep its purpose hidden from you? It confounds me . . ."

Geoffroi sighed, leaning back in his chair. "As I said, Ser Aaron, I cannot pretend to know their reasons. If you don't know, that is a further mystery. Whatever the case, I can tell you this: your arrival here is nothing short of divine providence."

"Divine providence?" Dumont scoffed, his tone dripping with sarcasm. "And how, exactly, do you figure that?" The cat suddenly hissed.

Ser Geoffroi looked sideways at the cat, hidden as it was in the shadow. "Damn cats. We keep them to kill the rats . . . never seen this one before." He grabbed an old paperweight from the table and launched it at the beast. But it was already gone.

Dumont's disapproving voice, Geoffroi 's exclamation, and the sound of the weight's impact on the stone wall drew my addled mind from the confines of its stupidity. It was starting to make sense: The Passage Knights. The cat's blue eyes. The message. Someone was looking out for us. Someone who had made it here ahead of us.

Edweene—it was now plain to see. I sighed in relief and could not suppress a small, self-deprecating laugh. The bird, the cat, Edweene—all are the same. I wondered about the depth of her sorcery. It was sacrilege, of course, but I'd put up with sacrilege for years now. Still, how far would her majyk go before it turned her soul as black as the art?

Geoffroi's gaze hardened as he watched my face, my mind working through the events of the night. I'd not been prudent in my exclamation or my expressions as I worked this out. I shook it away and looked hard at him. His eyes met mine, then flicked to the map on the table.

"A large force of the enemy, bearing many banners, is camped nearby. They have been scouring the area, their patrols growing bolder with each passing day. They look for something." He stared hard at me. It was an accusation. Then he continued, "If you had not arrived when you did, if I had not received that message, you would likely have been captured, or worse, as soon as you set foot in their lands."

His words sent a shiver down my spine. After everything we had been through, the thought of falling into the hands of the Gols was not something we would relish, to say the least, by The God. And it was always a danger. We knew the camp was here somewhere—but reckoned it further north in the woods. It is what we sought. But so close? That was not in our minds.

"And what do you propose we do now?" I asked. "It is The God's work, after all, and must not be delayed."

Geoffroi stood, his hands clasped behind his back. "I will guide you through the Golish-controlled territory. I know a safe route will allow us to avoid detection."

Dumont shook his head, his expression filled with disbelief or consternation. I could not tell which, and it gave me pause. He said, "We do not need twenty men girded in steel," his voice sharp with suspicion that I could not understand. "It will only slow us and likely alert the heathen."

Geoffroi's eyes narrowed, his jaw clenched tight. "You have no choice but to trust me, Ser Dumont. Without my aid, you will not make it past the Golish lines and into their lands—wherever you wish to go. I can assure you of that."

I glanced at Dumont, seeing the conflict playing out across his face. I trusted Geoffroi—at least to the extent that I believed he thought our mission was sanctioned. But having him along would complicate matters when things came to fruition. In that, Dumont was correct. But the strange, self-righteous outburst was unlike the reserved, disciplined knight. I couldn't shake the feeling that something was amiss, that something else was happening in Dumont's mind—something that concerned him greatly. And that concerned me.

"We will accept your aid," I said at last, my voice heavy with resignation. "But we need to alter the term, for The God wills it."

Dumont shot me an accusatory look as though taking The God's name in vain was some sacrilege. But he'd done worse on this trip, as had I. He had no place to speak.

"The God wills it," Geoffroi repeated and made the star on his chest. I did the same. Dumont hesitantly followed suit. Geoffroi continued, "Tell me, Ser, what it is you demand?"

"You cannot go with us, though I would have it so if it were up to me. My heart would have you with me, sword and shield, like old times. But it is by order of the King and The Bishop. This mission may not be revealed in any way. You read it yourself on the messenger's note. You must tell us where the enemy is, where his sentries are, and where this route of yours is. From there, we will find our way. And if we don't, it is God's will."

Geoffroi inclined his head, a grim, disdainful smile playing at the corners of his lips. "I understand, Ser. While I, too, would prefer to accompany you myself, I respect your need for discretion in this matter. The King's business is not for me to question."

He turned his attention to the map, his finger tracing a route through the treacherous terrain. "The Golish camp lies here," he said, tapping a spot deep within the Devil's Forest. "Their patrols are heaviest along this ridge and in the valley to the south. If you can avoid these areas, you will slip past undetected."

As he spoke, Dumont tapped restlessly on the table, and his brow furrowed deeper with each mention of the treacherous terrain ahead.

I leaned forward, studying the map intently. The route Geoffroi suggested was not an easy one, but it was far from impossible. With my skills as a former Dark Man and Edweene's uncanny abilities, I was confident we could navigate the dangers that lay ahead.

"And what of the path itself?" I asked, my eyes still fixed on the map. "Is it well-traveled, or will we be forging our own way?"

Geoffroi shook his head. "There is no path, Ser Aaron. Not one that any man has walked in living memory. You will be alone out there, with only your wits and steel to guide you. You will leave your horses, of course. They will get you killed."

That seemed to break Dumont. He nearly shouted, "The horses, by The God! We cannot." He pointed at the route we'd intended to take at the first, "There is a path here. We could take the mounts. We are knights. We will need—" Dumont began his tirade.

I held my hand up and shot him my most dangerous look. He stopped short and gave me a most angry glare. "I figured so, my lord," I said. "I remember the ground becomes too treacherous from here."

Geoffroi nodded. "It's true. But I know you, Aaron. And I have seen your grim work, by The God, at your worst. You can do this. It is your traveling companion and all his iron that concerns me."

"He is strong and fast. I have seen him fight. He will do well. And I can use . . . as you say . . . all that iron."

Dumont remained silent throughout the exchange. His expression became unreadable, but I could feel his anger and unease. To the man's credit, he held his tongue.

"We will need provisions," I said, returned to Geoffroi. "Food, water, and any other supplies you can spare. We travel light, but we must be prepared for any eventuality. It will take three days to get where we are going."

Geoffroi nodded, his mind working as he looked at the map. "Three days," he said. "Why, Ser, that would take you—"

"We will need provisions for six then, for we must return." I interrupted, putting his question to bed. He had figured out, rightly, that we were headed to the enemy's camp.

He said, "Of course. I will ensure that you have everything you need. And your beasts will be waiting when you return."

I stood and extended my hand in gratitude. "You have our thanks, Geoffroi. Your aid in this matter will not be forgotten."

He clasped my hand, his grip firm and strong. "Go with The God, Ser Aaron. May He watch over you and guide you to victory."

With that, he turned and strode from the room, leaving Dumont and me alone once more.

As soon as the door closed behind him, Dumont turned to me, his expression grave. "I don't like this, Aaron. We're walking into this unprotected and without our horses to aid our escape. Danger lurks. I would have the horses. I would take a different route. The most forthright route."

I sighed, running a hand through my hair. "What choice do we have, Dumont? We cannot abandon our mission when so much is at stake. And if we take the main route, we will die for sure. The God put us here. At this table. Your brother awaits, probably under whip and dagger point. The Gols' torture is extreme, you know?"

He shook his head, frustration etched into every line of his face. "And what of Edweene?

What if this is all some ploy, some scheme of hers to lead us astray?"

I felt a flicker of anger, but I pushed it aside. Edweene was the reason why we were not on the back of the Tawl's horse with sacks on our heads. "Edweene is not our enemy," I said, my voice firm. "She has risked everything to help and guide us on this path. I trust her. You should trust her."

Dumont said, "She stinks of abomination, Aaron. And you know it. I have no trust in her. And neither should you. Mark my words, Ser, if she betrays us, if any harm comes to us because of her . . . I will not hesitate to strike her down."

I met his gaze, my own eyes hard and unyielding. "It will not come to that, Dumont. I stake my life on it."

He held my gaze for a long moment, searching for any sign of doubt or hesitation. Finding none, he finally nodded, his shoulders slumping in resignation. "Then let us be on our way," he said. "The sooner we complete this cursed mission, the sooner we can put all of this behind us."

I couldn't help but agree with him. The weight of our task was heavy on my shoulders, and I was filled with dread at what lay ahead. But there was no turning back now. We had set our course, and we would see it through to the end, no matter the cost, by The God. I could not help thinking that the cost would be high. As we made our way back to the courtyard, I felt we were being watched. Occasionally, I caught glimpses of black flashes in the corners of my eye and glittering blue sparkles in crooks and rafters above.

Whatever dangers and betrayals lay ahead, we would not face them alone. Edweene would be with me, guiding us. With that knowledge, I felt renewed purpose and a steely determination to see our mission through to the end. I only wondered what had become of the Tawl.

CHAPTER 10
INTO THE DEVIL'S FOREST

The morning sun had barely begun to crest over the horizon when Dumont and I set out from Caer Gorak, our packs laden with supplies and our hearts heavy with the weight of our mission. Geoffroi saw us off at the gate, his expression grim as he clasped our hands in farewell.

"I do not know what you do, but I would go with you if I could," he said, his voice low and urgent. "The Gols are a formidable foe; they will do you badly if you are taken. So do not be taken, my friend. I have faith in you, Aaron. In both of you. May The God guide your steps and grant you victory."

With those parting words, we turned our backs on the fortress and struck out into the wilderness, leaving our horses behind. Their absence felt immediately strange, but I knew Geoffroi was right. Where we were going, horses would only slow us down and make us more vulnerable to detection.

The terrain was as treacherous as Geoffroi had warned. Twisted brushlands and stoney hills gave way to jagged outcroppings and steep ravines, each presenting its own set of challenges. We moved slowly and carefully, picking our way through the undergrowth and watching for any signs of the enemy.

As we walked, Dumont and I discussed our plan, going over the route Geoffroi had outlined.

"My brother depends on us," he said at one point, seemingly from nowhere. His voice was contemplative, and he appeared to be talking to himself. Some sort of argument in his own haunted head. We are all alone with our own thoughts on the eve of battle. It was no shame, no madness.

I said, "And we shall see him free from their grip. But we must remain vigilant, Dumont. Keep your eyes on the flanks. One can never know where the enemy waits."

It took him a moment to emerge from his reverie. Then he looked at me and said, "I should trust your main Geoffroi to take us away from the enemy's ambuscade, now?" Of course, he made light of my decision to follow the man's directions instead of running headlong through the obvious route. I went quiet, choosing not to engage in such petty arguing. Whichever route we took, it behooved us to be on our guard. Dumont knew this. Any argument was pointless.

By nightfall, we were on the rim of Devil's Forest, surrounded by towering trees that closed around us like a prison gate. Tomorrow would find us deep inside. We found a small, secluded clearing inside the forest, which was truly just a thinner spot in the constricting trees, and set up camp.

"I will take the first watch," I said to Dumont as we dropped rucks and gear on the ground. The jagged rocks were already giving way to clumpy, stone-infested earth covered with weeds and un-dergrowth. If my memory held true, it would turn to thick briars and thorny brush on the morrow. At least we slept on better ground tonight, such as it was.

"Wake me in two hours, if you will," he an-swered, lying on his back with his head on his rucksack.

"Done," I said and nodded. But he was already asleep.

The sound of Dumont's light snoring lulled me to an in-between place—in between sleep and awareness. I was awake, going through my mo-tions, watching the darkness for Gols or creeping monstrosities known to lurk in this wood, yet my eyes drifted closed, and my head bobbed. The world around me became blurred and insub-stantial—a waking dreamland. How much was this place? And how much was my exhaustion from days on the road? I stood to clear the cob-webs, shook my arms, and paced, picking my way through the thickening brush around the camp. I did my best to remain quiet, creeping like I was trained in the Dark Men—slowly, deliberately, one foot in front of the other—ball of the foot first, then finding the heel and settling it quietly. Every few steps, I stopped and crouched, eyes into the dark.

The forest was alive and dangerous. I could feel it—as though it wanted us gone, dead. This was a place of dark sorcery. Legends and stories told by the Abbot in our local house of worship back home told that this is where Abominations and Sorcerers drew their power. It all originated here. I thought it was bunk, really. Other stories said the same of the Blightwood far to the north or the Golspire Mountains. Whatever the case, it was definitely true that there was something here, something ominous. And so, I took my time, watched, and listened, and observed.

Midway through the watch; the slightest sound drifted to my ears—unnatural and distinct from the natural sounds around me, no matter how twisted and blighted they might be—the sound of branches sliding off leather or other material. I lowered myself behind a thick bough and sidestepped to be able to reach Dumont in a rush or with a thrown pebble if needs be. The sound came again, and I looked in its direction. I saw nothing. Whoever—whatever—it was, they were trained and experienced in the stalk. But they were facing a Dark Man, and few were more competent than we at such matters.

I slid a little more in the direction of the camp, making sure to keep enough natural cover between me and this sound to maximize my chances of hiding, and slid my knife from its scabbard ever so quietly. My heart was racing, and my breath was starting to come in short. I breathed deeply to control it and focused on the enemy that stalked me. Calm. Deliberate movements. Don't panic. Don't jump. Wait, watch, and keep moving.

A figure materialized out of the shadows like a ghost, some five paces distant. I clenched my dagger and contemplated my killing strike: quick rush forward, force their weapon arm outside, body positioned inside any strike, and drive my dagger up under the ribs. The figure was facing me and shorter than me. It crouched and slid forward, moving like a cat, graceful and lethal. By the movements, my stroke would have to be perfect, or I'd be the one on my back, bleeding out. Fortunately, despite the darkness, I recognized the deadly movements almost immediately. And just as quickly pushed away my plans for murder. It was Edweene.

"Peace, Aaron," she said, her voice low and soothed. She'd seen me all along. "I come bearing news."

I relaxed my grip on my weapon, but only slightly. "Edweene. Damn. I almost killed you."

"I know. I watched you. You forget the benefits my curse gives me."

"I forgot nothing. I did not know it was you. We have got to work out a signal."

She laughed quietly. "We should at that."

I whispered, "What news?"

She stepped in close and placed her hand on my knee as I knelt. A jolt ran through my back. I caught my breath, but her expression was troubled. She ignored my reaction. "Aaron, the Tawl has escaped my grasp. He is a slippery bastard, always one step ahead. He met agents at the ford and slipped by the fortress. Had, I not intervened, he would have been waiting for you."

"Thank you," I whispered. "Sounds like you saved us."

"I made an attempt, Aaron. I am always on your side, even when we oppose each other. It is odd, but such things are possible. We can be allies, no matter the situation."

"We are . . . my lady. Allies, I mean."

"I fear your friend does not agree."

"Dumont is a powerful and dangerous knight. It is best we manage him. He will be a good ally, too. He fights very well."

"I'm not so sure, Aaron. He makes me nervous. And that competent blade work may well be turned on us, by the end of this endeavor."

"You two are enemies—deep in your hearts. You have convinced yourselves of it. As you and I once did. That is hard to overcome. He is the Crusader, a virtuous Knight of the Star. You are—"

"An Abomination. I know." Her voice was filled with hurt.

"The cat," I said and laughed, trying to change the subject. "That is new to me."

She said nothing meaningful about it, just hinted at newfound strengths since we last campaigned together: "I have found I possess abilities with the creatures of the dead, harbingers of curses, and black things that roam the underworld. I found this when I was done in by Ser Gavreaux's Treachery."

Discussing Gavreaux, and my allegiance to him would only upset matters worse, so I passed the comment by. And the mention of her powers always disconcerted me. Every time we spoke, it seemed that some new dark sorcery had revealed itself. She was a manifestation of all the things The God despised. It put distance between us, despite my unholy attraction to her, my connection. I asked tentatively, not really wanting an answer, "Is that all? Are there other things—"

"A woman is allowed some secrets, Aaron. Is she not?" Her blue eyes sparkled, and she smiled playfully.

"Indeed, she is, my lady," I said. "I suppose now is not the time for such things, though. We'll be on the camp in two days, if Geoffroi's directions are to be trusted. I would have some reconnais-sance . . . if you are willing."

She stopped and smiled, then turned suddenly serious. "I will find a way to guide you to your destination. No promises, though, Aaron. This cursed place is ripe with the enemy."

As she spoke the words, she flinched unex-pectedly and grasped her side. And I noticed the way she held herself, the slight hitch in her breathing that spoke of pain and injury. All things, in my haste to connect or talk to her, I'd overlooked. You're hurt," I said, taking a step toward her.

She waved off my concern. "It is nothing. A scratch, naught more. I will heal."

But I could see the truth in her eyes, how she favored her left side and the pallor of her already pale skin. She was badly wounded. "This is not like you. When did—"

"Aaron, I am fine. It happened yesterday. In my melee with the Tawl, we exchanged wounds," she laughed darkly. "Though he may have gotten the better of it, he likely limps, as well."

"Edweene . . ." I began, but she cut me off with a shake of her head.

"There is no time for that now—not in these woods. I am more alive here, you know. I am closer to the place that forged me. And so, I heal more akin to you. But it is meaningless. My wounds do not change the need."

The place of which she spoke was no geography, no locale on the map. It was the underworld. She was closer here to the underworld. The thought was sobering. I was quiet while I watched her. Concern was heavy in my mind. My heart pounded at the thought of this woman damaged—for me. A feeling of anxiousness buzzed in my chest. I knew if I spoke, she'd chastise me, however. So, I remained quiet. Instinctively, I reached out a hand.

She batted it away and gave me an angry glare. "Listen to me, Aaron. In the days to come, watch for my raven. Follow its lead, and it will guide you true. Trust in it as you trust in me. If you cannot see it, look for marks or signs, or the black cat. You will know."

I nodded and made to speak, to ask questions. But she didn't wait. With those cryptic words, she vanished into the shadows, leaving me alone with my thoughts, my growing concern over her health, and the weight of our mission pressing down upon me.

*

Darkness was still heavy on the land, when we set out once more. That is not to say that it was night, for in this place, the thick canopy let the night drag on for hours after the sun rose. Dawn came late, and twilight would come early. Our path took us deeper into the heart of the forest. The Devil's Forest was oppressive, the darkness, heavy branches, and thick, spiny leaves pushing down on us from above. Many times, we'd lose our way as we skirted impenetrable briars and thickets. The going was slow, and the terrain became more treacherous with each step. This, according to Geoffroi was the pathway to follow, but at times it seemed a fabrication. This could be no path . . . could it? Dumont was not a man to complain, but on more than one occasion, he let me know his thoughts.

"Damn! By The God, Aaron, why do we persist in this madness? Do you even know where we are?" he asked as he swatted one particularly stickery vine from his face. His skin was gleaming with sweat, and scratches had risen across his cheeks and arms. By then, he'd removed most of his armor in the pursuit of comfort and wore naught but his breastplate. He'd packed the rest in a bag he carried on his back. His helmet hung from his shoulder by a leather strap.

"Trust me, Dumont, this is a path. The Devil's Forest is thick and dangerous. The path we take now is as clear as it gets. It is leading us where we need to go. If we thought the way you do, we'd be ambushed for sure. Everyone avoids the thickets and briars. They'd expect us at every turn if we took our planned route. Trust me—and lord Geoffroi—in this matter. This is the way." I spoke as confidently as I could. The forest was actually thicker than I remembered, and it was giving me concern that Dumont was right—that, somehow, we'd strayed from our path.

"Clear as it gets? Path? Surely you mock me, Aaron."

"I would not, Dumont," I said. "But, we'd best hurry." I said. I was constantly looking skyward for Edweene's Raven. Hoping for her to confirm my course. But the trees made it difficult. Still, I felt the creature's eyes upon us. It was not until the sun was high in the sky, and we were about to break for our mid-day meal, that I spotted it. We slipped out of a thick grouping of thorny trees, and the sky opened a sliver above. There, the raven was circling, its black wings stark against the pale gray sky. It circled once, twice, then veered off to the east, disappearing into the trees. Without a word, I followed, trusting in Edweene's promise.

Dumont fell into step beside me, his expression quizzical. Should we stop to eat?" he asked. "I'm famished and we need to renew our energy after this rough march."

"Soon, Dumont. Soon. Just a bit further." The truth was, I had no idea how much further. But, I pressed ahead, not wanting to lose the raven's track.

But the forest opened a little, and the track became somewhat obvious—not in the way one might follow an animal trail, but in the way that one part of the forest might be less vegetated than another, and it followed roughly the direction the bird had winged away.

"Where are we going?" he asked, his voice low and wary. "You seem all fired excited to be moving quickly now, as though you've got some renewed energy."

It was true, but only because I had a direction now, and my confidence was boosted. I didn't answer, my gaze fixed on the path ahead. I knew how it looked to him, like I was chasing ghosts and shadows, but I trusted in Edweene. And when your lych signaled for you to move, you moved.

As we pressed on, the raven reappeared, always just ahead of us, mostly obscured in tree limbs and blighted leaves, leading us through a maze of hidden paths and concealed trails. Dumont marveled at my apparent sixth sense, my uncanny ability to navigate the treacherous terrain. But I said nothing of the raven or Edweene's guidance. I knew he would not approve.

It was that guidance that saved us from disaster more than once. As we neared a narrow ravine, the ground was falling quickly before us, and the lighter brush led the way into the low ground. On either side of us, the land began to rise in wide, funnel like terrain feature, choked on the edges with thick trees and heavy briars. It was the natural way to proceed. It was also a natural point to funnel an enemy. Before we entered that funnel too deeply, the raven suddenly changed course, veering sharply to the right. I followed without hesitation, into the thicker brush. Dumont was close at my heels, cursing my seemingly mad course change.

It wasn't until we had put some distance between ourselves and the ravine mouth that we heard voices, the clank of armor and weapons. We crouched and went silent, struggling our way through the thick brush toward the noise, doing our best to remain silent. I signaled Dumont to leave his ruck and bag, and I slipped mine into some low briars, out of sight. We crept forward, peering over the edge of a ravine cut into the rocky terrain. The ravine was crowded with thick brush, and two-men's height in depth. At the bottom, a group of six Golish soldiers—six that we could see—had set up an ambush—likely for game, pig, or bear or some such—deep in the brush. Their spears were set towards the mouth of the ravine. Behind toward the mouth of the ravine, we heard more—likely those that would drive the game to be killed.

We had come close to walking straight into that gulch. If not for the raven's warning, we would have been captured or killed—or at least had to fight our way out or through the heathens—and our mission might well have been over before it had truly begun.

We pressed on, the raven guiding us ever closer to our goal. As the sun began to set on the second day, we knew we were drawing near to the Golish camp. The signs were unmistakable. Trampled underbrush, and discarded remnants of meals and campsites gave us ample warning. It seems the Golish regulars were not concerned with policing their whereabouts.

The ravine was far behind, but the route that took the warriors to their hunting ground was no doubt close at hand. So, we moved more slowly, our intention to be stealthy, not quick. I led five paces ahead of Dumont, who, after the encounter at the gorge, was properly chastised and moved more quietly. His complaining and admonitions toward me were left behind with the realization that I was a competent ranger and woodsman.

But, as darkness dropped on us, I saw ahead of me a movement in the brush. A lone Gol warrior, clad in a scale-armored surcoat and conical helm, walked slowly along a path that ran roughly perpendicular to our trek. He carried a spear in his hands, and wore his scimitar on his hip. He seemed to be alone. I surmised he was patrolling the perimeter of a camp. His eyes were wary and he watched from left to right. He'd stopped. Maybe he heard something—us?

I signaled Dumont, and we froze. I lowered myself until the brush fully covered me, and Dumont behind me, wisely did likewise. The sentry was close—perhaps twenty paces, and if he was not wearing his helmet and coif he could probably have heard us.

And so I barely dared to breathe.

The man paused, his hand grip on the spear tightening as he lowered it and pointed it into the trees, keeping it pointed in the direction of his body as he quietly turned and searched the wood. For a moment, I feared he had spotted us. Then, he turned and continued his patrol, moving away from our position, slowly and deliberately, watching and listening as he went.

I let out a slow, measured breath. My heart hammered in my chest.

And suddenly Dumont was next to me. He had slid up as I watched. "Do we need to take him out?" he whispered, his mouth only inches from my ear, and his voice barely audible. "Quietly, before he raises the alarm."

I shrugged, my mind racing as I worked through a plan in my head. We couldn't afford to be reckless, not when we were so close to our goal. I had no idea how close the camp was. But a single sentry told me it was very close. Which meant, we'd lost any option to circle around, lest we wanted to double back. But we didn't know where the hunting party was either, or they might well come upon us, so that was not a good option either.

But if we killed him, would he be missed? I thought so.

None of the options before us was good. I decided to retreat, in a direction nearly perpendicular to where we'd come from to avoid the hunting party. That would take us further from our goal, but it would be safer. We could wait for tomorrow, camped deep in the wood where we could avoid detection by the camp's sentries, wherever that camp was, and the hunting party when it likely returned tonight. Most importantly, perhaps we could facilitate a reconnaissance when things got dark.

That, I decided, was the best plan.

I motioned for Dumont to circle around to the right for a few paces, then into the woods. He nodded, relief on his face. I gave him a thin-lipped smile. We crept in that direction, my footsteps silent on the forest floor. I thought the sentry was behind, out of sight, his back turned to us as he made his way along his track. But suddenly, I realized there was another. Another sentry loomed out of the wood in front of us, spear held over his shoulders in a hap-hazard, lazy manner that luckily was normal for undisciplined troops in their own territory.

He stopped. I stopped. Our eyes met. His eyes widened in surprise as he saw me emerging from the shadowy brush. For a moment, he stood there, frozen in a tableau of tension and anticipation. Without hesitation, I drew my knife. The blade glinted in the fading light, like coming death. And I rushed him.

CHAPTER 11

SHADOWS OF DOUBT

The Gol's eyes widened in surprise. I lunged forward. My knife flashed. The blade found its mark, slipping between the gaps in the sentry's coif and piercing his throat. The man let out a gurgling, moaning cry. He grasped at the wound as he collapsed to the ground, and blood pumped through his fingers and over his chest and face.

The kill was as silent as it could be. This is one thing at which I excel—killing quickly, silently. I crouched, holding my gloved hand over his mouth to keep him silent. As is my way, I avoided his eyes until he expired. Such things haunted me, and I needed no more of that.

I moved quickly, dragging the body into the undergrowth out of sight and moving the brush and dirt around to cover what trace of the kill I could. Dumont appeared at my side, his blade drawn and ready. We exchanged a tense look, knowing that someone would likely notice the sentry's absence soon.

"We need to move," I whispered, wiping my blade clean on the sentry's surcoat. "The camp can't be far."

Dumont nodded, his eyes scanning the surrounding forest.

"Should we just go in? We still can surprise them," he recommended, his voice hard and even resigned.

"I think that's a fool's notion, Dumont," I said, not meaning to impugn the man's intelligence. And he did not take it that way from the look on his face. I continued, "There are hundreds. We'd be killed without a plan. And quickly. We should find a safe place to regroup and plan our next move," I said.

"Not now, soon. Tonight, before his—"

"Let's go, Dumont," I said. I was bewildered at his attachment to this suicidal idea.

We retreated deeper into the woods, separating ourselves from the Golish camp. The sun had nearly set, and the shadows grew long and dark beneath the twisted boughs. After a half-hour of careful progress, we found a small, sheltered hollow, hidden from view by a thick wall of thorny bushes.

I kneeled, using my dagger to clear a small patch of earth. "We need to scout the camp, get a better idea of what we're up against."

Dumont agreed, settling down beside me. "We should wait until full dark. Move in quietly, see what we can learn about their numbers, defenses, and where they might hold Prenot."

I agreed, and we dumped our gear and readied the camp, making sure we appropriately camouflaged everything before we left. I assured Dumont that I could find our way back later on, when it was dark. So, we rested for a time, eating a meager meal of hard bread and dried meat from our packs. As the last light faded from the sky, we waited another hour, then set out, ghosting through the undergrowth toward where we believed the Golish camp was located.

It was easy to find. We could smell their campfires long before we reached it. After some time, we found much evidence of activity in the area—many paths that led toward the camp. Some large, some small, some almost impossible to find. The camp was larger than expected, with dozens of tents and crude shelters arranged around a central fire pit in a rough circle. Sentries patrolled the perimeter, weaving in and out of the thick brush as they did, their spears glinting in the flickering light of the flames. Dumont and I crept closer, using the shadows and the dense foliage to remain unseen.

Tents and banners loomed out of the morning gloom as the woods began to thin out sufficiently to facilitate a bivouac. I squatted amongst a particularly heavy briar patch fifty feet from the edge of the encampment and motioned for my companion to come up. Soon, Dumont squatted next to me. He was getting better at moving silently. I found that satisfying, for some reason. He put his hand on my back. "From here, we can see most of the camp," he whispered, his voice carrying in the darkness, "but some disappear amongst those trees." He pointed off to the right, some distance.

I nodded. "Right now, let's just settle for a bit. Watch."

"Right," he said, settling in on the back of his feet, sliding to a seated position. "Wait and watch. Brave knights are we," he added sarcastically.

I ignored his barb and continued my vigil. We spent nearly an hour observing the camp, counting the sentries, and studying the layout. At some point, Dumont rose to kneeling and became more attentive, much to my appreciation. One never quite feels respected when the person he's supposed to go into battle with isn't giving it the appropriate respect and attention. But Dumont was a man who wanted to act. In his mind, this subterfuge was below him. But his way would likely be suicide. He must have known that when we'd left the Stone all those days ago. It seemed strange that he was so unsettled by our plans of stealth. Regardless, he paid attention now, and we focused on a large, heavily guarded tent near the center of the encampment, reasoning that it was the most likely place for a high-value prisoner like Ser Prenot to be held.

The inaction was influencing me as well; I cannot deny it. I was having remembrances of a time when I entered a camp, much like this one, to rescue Edweene and destroy the sorcerer Kah Fau and the dreaded Golish general Ek Inir Ahn. It was dangerous. Perhaps more dangerous than this one, which sets these very events in motion. Now, here I was again. It seemed this war never changed. Killing, sneaking, rescuing. It was a bloody cycle that I could not seem to escape.

As we crouched there in that wood, noting the comings and goings, so focused were we on our task that we did not notice the sound of Golish warriors' harsh, guttural voices erupting from the far side of the camp until it was almost too late. It shattered the eerie stillness of the night and pierced the air, sending my heart to thunder. My breath caught, and my head snapped in that direction. Dumont began to stand and draw steel, but I grabbed his arm, stopping that mad notion. The sound of heavy footfalls and the rustling of underbrush nearby forced my heart further into my throat. It took a moment, but I soon divined what was happening: the hunting party had returned.

And they were dangerously close to our position.

I exchanged a glance with Dumont, who now half-stood, hand on the pommel. We both froze, hardly daring to breathe. The Golish warriors emerged from the forest like specters, their faces painted with the blood of their kills, their bronze skin illuminated by the flickering campfires. They dragged the carcasses of several large boars behind them, the animals' lifeless eyes staring blankly into the void—that would be us if we acted impulsively now.

I tugged on Dumont's arm, and he lowered himself. With a silent, concurring look, we slid silently up, closer into the briars.

They were mere feet away. The odor of sickly body odor from days in the field and the ruptured gore from their kills clung to their bodies in disgusting clouds. The closer they got, the deeper I pressed into the shadows. I gripped the hilt of my sword so tightly that my knuckles turned white. Beside me, Dumont was as still as a statue, his face a grim mask of determination.

An eternity seemed to pass as the party made their way into the camp, their voices fading into the night. Only when the last of them had disappeared did I allow myself to breathe again, my heart pounding in my ears like a drum that slowly relented to a dull thud.

Wordlessly, Dumont and I retreated to our hidden hollow, the adrenaline still coursing through our veins. It was an additional complication. The hunting party's return would raise the camp's awareness as they dealt with their game, put away their gear, reported in, and prepared for sleep. Our task had become more difficult.

With trembling hands, I used my dagger to scratch a rough map of the camp on the rough earth, my mind racing as I tried to recall every detail of what we had seen. Dumont joined me, his own blade carving out the location of the central tent, the sentries' patrol routes, and the potential entry points we had identified. But even as we worked, I couldn't shake the feeling of nervousness that had settled over me. The hunting party's return had been a reminder of the dangers we faced and that unknowns were constantly a factor. Nothing was guaranteed, and death lurked where we did not expect it.

"It won't be easy," I said, studying the crude map. "But if we can create a distraction, draw the sentries away from that central tent, we might have a chance. But I don't like that idea much either. A distraction could raise the general alarm."

Dumont nodded; his brow furrowed in thought. "We could set fire to one of the other tents, draw them all away. Everyone. It would wake them, but, perhaps—"

He was interrupted by a sudden rustling in the brush behind us. We both spun around, blades drawn, ready to face whatever threat had found us. Edweene stepped out of the shadows instead of a Golish warrior, her blue eyes glinting in the darkness. I knew immediately she'd meant for us to hear her. Edweene does not alert her enemies—or friends—if she doesn't wish to.

Dumont had different ideas. He reacted instantly, lunging forward with his sword. Edweene sidestepped the blow, her own blade flashing up to block his follow-up strike. I leaped between them, my arms outstretched to keep them apart.

"Stop!" I hissed, glaring at Dumont. "She's not our enemy."

Dumont hesitated. His sword was still raised and pointed directly at Edweene. "She startled me," he said, his voice tight with suspicion. "I thought she was one of the enemy, a heathen fallen upon us as we were unprepared."

Edweene's eyes narrowed, and I saw distrust and anger simmering beneath the surface. There was no doubt in my mind what she suspected—that Dumont had recognized her and used the darkness as an excuse for his aggression.

"If I was your enemy, you'd both be dead, I assure you." She stated flatly.

"I doubt such, witch," he responded. "You may have been able to slip in a strike or two," he admitted, "but in the end, it's my steel that would have ended the fight."

"You misunderstand me, Ser," she scoffed. "You'd have been dead before the fight. I've been watching you for some time." His eyes widened, but she went on. "Regardless, Aaron . . ." she looked at me, "I come bearing information," Edweene said, her gaze then flashing to Dumont. ". . . about your brother, Ser Prenot. It is relevant to your—our—plan."

As she spoke, I noticed her wounds appeared to have healed. She no longer favored her side, and she stood, as she always had, graceful and deadly as she spoke. This healing of hers was disconcerting. How? And what fueled it? I don't know. I only knew that all these things came to her with a cost. I swallowed my concern. She'd not have any of it anyway. I gestured for her to continue.

But, before she could, Dumont interrupted. His voice was harsh. "Where have you been? Why appear now, after leaving us for so long?"

To her credit, Edweene ignored his insinuations. She turned to me. "You have the wrong location," she said, pointing to the map we had drawn. "Ser Prenot is being held here, in this tent to the west." Using the point of her curved sword, she marked the tent.

I frowned, looking closer at the spot she indicated. It was smaller and less heavily guarded than the central tent we had identified. "How do you know this?"

Edweene hesitated, and I could see the calculation in her eyes. The lych could see better in the dark, but she would not reveal that to Dumont without risking an outright attack. And I would never betray her.

"I have my ways," she said finally, her tone brooking no argument. "Trust me, as you always have."

Dumont scoffed, his suspicion plain. "Trust you? For all we know, you could be leading us into a trap," he turned to me. "This feels wrong," he said. "She feels wrong. Why should we believe her reconnaissance is better than ours? We watched for hours."

I held up my hand, silencing the knight's protests. "It is a good question, Edweene. And one I think comes in good faith."

She glared at me, her eyes narrowing.

"But I'll not belabor this conversation anymore. Nor question your honor, or loyalty to me. Your scouting skills are better than mine. I have much experience with this, Dumont . . ." I let that all sink in. I saw the knight's disbelief plain on his face. I continued before he could put up too much of a fight. "We will follow Edweene's plan," I said, my voice firm. "She has never led us astray before."

Dumont held his tongue. The tension between the three of us hung like a gray haze, heavy and poisoning—a simmering undercurrent of mistrust and unspoken accusations.

"Let's prepare," I finally said. We'll go in three hours when they are all most exhausted and asleep, and morning is only an hour away. It is dark, and you may wish for a rest.

We spent the next hour revising our plan, incorporating Edweene's new information. She provided valuable insights, drawing on her unique abilities to help us identify the camp's defense weaknesses and the best approach for the mission.

Despite the uneasy truce, I could feel Dumont's eyes on us, watching for any sign of betrayal. The knight's loyalty to the Crusade was unwavering, and his suspicion of Edweene was born of a lifetime of training and indoctrination. This conflict between them was not over. And I had a dark premonition of how it would end. After we completed the plan, we gathered what supplies and equipment we could from our limited resources. We sharpened our blades, checked our armor, and ran through the plan again and again, committing every detail to memory.

Finally, we settled into rest. Again, I took the first watch, scanning the surrounding forest for any sign of trouble. Dumont fell to sleep after slinking into the brush where we could not see him easily.

I went to Edweene, and she watched me come. I wanted to reach out and pull her in, but I knew that was not possible. That desire had been rebuked the day before we killed the necromancer when I felt she'd almost died in my arms. It was, of course, torture she'd endured then. She couldn't die without losing her phylactery. And she wore that ring on her finger. I could see it glittering, even now, when it was so dark. She smiled at me.

"You are well and healed, I see," I whispered.

"Aaron, you need your sleep. Sleep, I will watch." She turned sideways to me, so any foolish attempt to embrace her would have failed. But I was not foolish anymore when it came to Edweene—at least not openly so.

"Okay . . ." I slipped away to a place I'd cleared and lay down.

The specifics of the plan played through my mind as I slipped into sleep. It seemed I'd only just closed my eyes when Edweene shook me awake.

"Aaron, you must awaken. Dumont is gone."

As she said it, a cold knot of fear settled in my gut as I realized the implications of Dumont's disappearance. Edweene stood by, arms folded, and watched as I jumped up and rushed to where he had put his bedroll. It was gone. So was all his gear. I stared numbly at the matted-down grass and pushed aside rocks where he'd presumably made his bed. Had he abandoned us, unwilling to trust in Edweene's plan? Or had he struck out on his own, determined to rescue Ser Prenot himself and claim the glory?

And Edweene watched. "You don't believe me, Aaron? He is gone."

"I did not say that Edweene," I responded but kept up my little search. As I examined the little hollow for any sign of struggle or foul play, a darker thought crept into my mind. Could Edweene have dispatched Dumont while I slept, hiding the body to eliminate the threat of his suspicion and mistrust?

I glanced at the nun, her blue eyes glowing in the predawn gloom. She met my gaze, and for a moment, I thought I saw a flicker of guilt or uncertainty there. But it was gone in an instant, replaced by the steel I had come to know so well.

"Did you see where, when he left?" I asked her. The lych didn't sleep. She should have seen anything.

"I did not, Aaron. That is not an accusation I hear, is it?" Not waiting for me to answer, she pulled up her mouth in a smile. "Whatever the case, his departure is less than honorable. Hardly knightly, at all." She scoffed.

I shook my head and pushed the thought aside. Edweene was many things, but she was not a cold-blooded killer. She had proven her loyalty to me time and time again, and I would not let Dumont's disappearance sow the seeds of doubt between us. I couldn't. if he was indeed gone, she was my only ally in this madness. Prenot had to be freed—and more importantly, the bishop had to be brought to account.

Now, that mission had become twofold more complicated.

Again.

We packed up our meager camp and prepared to set out, and I was unable to shake the feeling that something was amiss, something deeper than Dumont leaving to attempt the rescue on his own—fool that he might be. It seemed madness. Dumont's absence hung over me like a dark portent of fractures and fault lines in our uneasy alliance—even my connection to Edweene's. Could an abomination really be trusted?

Yes. I told myself. *She can be. She must be.*

But even as I fortified myself for the trials to come, I wondered if that trust would be enough.

CHAPTER 12
BETRAYAL

The first light of dawn was a few long hours away. It was the coldest time of night but the one that spoke of the coming day. Soon the woods would be alive, teeming with the creatures that lived here. But it brought no comfort for Edweene and me, huddled together in the shadows of the Devil's Forest. Only tension as we worked against a schedule. There was no time to delay. The darkness was our ally, our shield against the defenses that lurked within the Golish camp—and now, with Dumont on the wing, we were that much more pressed for time. And, as we spoke in hushed tones, the weight of Dumont's disappearance lay upon us like a suffocating shroud.

"We can't just leave him out there," I growled, my brow furrowed with a mixture of concern and frustration.

Edweene's eyes flashed in the gloom. Her patience with my overdone concern wore thin. She'd always been practical, able to force such things away. Deal with what is in front of her. I'd done it, too, but lamented my grievances too openly. I wore my heart upon my sleeve, so to speak. It was not a positive feature. "He made his choice, Aaron. He left us, remember? We have a duty to fulfill, and time is running out. Ser Prenot's life hangs in the balance. And with it, so does your mission—this intelligence you seem to need to discredit the bishop."

"I know this, lych," I responded, twisting the word slightly. It was unfair and selfish, but sometimes, I wanted her to feel what I struggled with. And I, fairly or not, often attributed her lack of empathy to her abomination.

She looked at me, her blue eyes intense, narrowed. There it was—the pain. "Aaron," she began, then lapsed into silence and seemed to consider what she said. "We do not need to rescue this knight, Prenot. We could exact a measure of vengeance on the bishop. Leave here. Kill him. That simple."

Practical. Always practical. I'd hurt her, with my comment, but she'd pushed that away and focused on the simplistic view of things. Deal with the problem before you. She was right. But I wanted my life, a life. Killing the bishop would put me at odds with the Church of the Star, The God, the Crusade, and, most of all, my people far away in Rivershire. And I wasn't a Dark Man anymore was I? And the mention of Ser Prenot sent a twist of guilt through my gut. The young knight's fate was a constant reminder of the stakes we faced, the price of failure etched in blood and bone. Did he deserve to perish here alone, abandoned by The God?

"Edweene, we must free this knight—"

"Stop, Aaron. You are a hypocrite—or worse. Just weeks ago, you'd have abandoned that man for your doomed mission to speak to the king and unearth evidence in Clurak, and now—is it some matter of honor?"

I stared at her. Although I couldn't counter this argument, we were here now, and it became a matter of honor. I felt the need to complete this. And I still wanted to know what Prenot knew about the bishop—and now, I needed to know the state of Dumont. He had undertaken this fool's errant because of his distrust for my companion. And now, he put our entire mission in jeopardy for his misplaced honor. I could not simply let him die in a Gol camp. The thought of abandoning him to an unknown fate was unconscionable to me.

"Enough," I said. "I do not disagree. I am, and always have been, a conflicted soul. But time is limited, and we must be away. I would rescue this knight. I would find Dumont. I ask that you be with me in this Edweene. I beg it."

Every moment we delayed brought Ser Prenot closer to a grim end. With a heavy sigh, I nodded, the decision weighing on my shoulders like a leaden cloak.

"I am with you, Ser," she said, squaring up to me, hands on her hips. She stared hard at me. "Of course I am."

"We proceed then with the rescue," I said, my voice steady despite the turmoil. "Dumont is a skilled warrior and a true knight. We must trust in his abilities and believe that The God will guide him back to us. But Ser Prenot's life is our priority, and we cannot fail him."

Edweene's gaze softened, and a flicker of understanding passed between us. She placed a hand on my shoulder, a welcome gesture of support and solidarity. "We'd best hurry, then," she said.

Together, we melted into the shadows, our footsteps silent as we made our way toward the Golish camp. We knew the track by now, but it was still rough going. We did not want to leave a pathway to our camp. Vines, stickers, and briars bit at our skin, and sharp rocks assailed our boots as we slipped through the wood. I'd left my steel back at the camp, save my long knife and dagger. We needed to move swiftly, and all that gear would slow us. There was a price, of course, and that was protection—from the weapons of our enemies and the nasty, thorny undergrowth in the Devil's Forest. I'm sure Edweene had a faster way to move, one more attuned to her sorcery, but she stayed with me. I was grateful for that, at least.

As we drew closer, the stench of unwashed bodies and the coppery tang of blood once again assaulted my nostrils, a visceral reminder of the enemy that awaited us. In the blackness, we moved with stealth, like mere ghosts. We slipped between the sentries, now lost in the haze of their exhaustion, and passed the first line of ragged tents and sleeping places. We darted from tent to tent, Edweene leading the way, avoiding the flickering orange light thrown out from the watch fires and torches that cast strange, spooky shadows about. I kept over watch as she moved from cover to cover, and she turned and watched as I followed across the danger areas. We kept our eyes open for Dumont. He had to be doing the same. He would be loud, and blundering, not a skilled assassin, as we were. But we saw nothing, heard nothing, of the knight. And so, we continued, our breath misting in the morning air, labored as we were from the exertion.

When we had closed half the distance to the tent identified by Edweene, we heard the guttural laughter of Golish warriors, amplified in the night's silence. At least some were awake. It was a stark reminder to be careful and take nothing for granted. And still, there was no sign of our knightly companion.

Navigating the labyrinthine camp was like walking through the maw of an abominable beast, the tent where our enemies laired, were its terrifying teeth. Danger seemed to lurk everywhere. Noises: breathing, whispered voices, creaking of equipment and the flapping of banners and tarpaulins, and tent flaps in the breeze, awakening birds and the snorts of distant horses of the cavalry seemed to make the place a living beast, into which we had somehow come to be devoured.

At one point, Edweene found herself face to face with two Golish warriors, their eyes bleary with drink, confused, and listless. They'd come from behind a tent, through which I had no visibility and too much distance. I thought perhaps they'd dismiss her and move on, but one recognized her as a threat after a moment of uncertainty. He dropped his wine skin and fumbled for his weapon, leaning on his drunken companion as he did. My long knife was in my hand instantly.

But Edweene was close and faster. Her voice rose low and melodic and infernal. I stared as she reached out to them, her left hand outstretched in some mal-formed clawlike horror as she did. The warriors' eyes glazed over, their bodies going slack as they slumped to the ground, lost in an enchanted slumber—or that is what I told myself.

I shot Edweene a horrified look. She glared back at me and pressed on, signaling the bodies as she did. I had no desire to touch these two things, cursed now as they were with black sorcery. But I understood the pressing matter of the thing. I'd done things, questionable things I was afraid to do before. This would be no different. I dragged them the short distance behind a nearby rack of rudimentary spears and polearms as she watched from beyond, her blue eyes glittering dangerously. I hoped only that curses were not like diseases, and I would not be tainted.

At last, we neared the tent where Edweene had told us Ser Prenot was being held, its dark silhouette looming like a shadow against the gray backdrop of the dark forest and silent camp, cast as it was in the glowing orange of a nearby watch fire. We crouched behind an armorer's table some ten feet distant and at an oblique angle to the two guards standing at the structure's front entrance. Heavy boxes, bags, and the wall of a makeshift cavalry stable blocked the back and sides of the structure. There was no way to slice our way in through sides or flank.

To my left was a peddle-powered sharpening stone, a body's width away. The ground between us and our quarry was an open, well-traveled trail camp thoroughfare. The two guards held their spears in the manner that complacent men do: one leaned heavily on his as though it was all that kept him from falling, and the other had leaned his weapon against the tent like it was a put-away broomstick. They both wore short, curved blades at their waists, and had we been able to see their eyes from this angle, they would likely have been dull and tired if they were open at all.

Edweene and I exchanged glances, a silent understanding passing between us. Slowly, we moved to the left, getting the tent between us and the guards. I signaled to Edweene to move to the right, around the stables, and come at the second guard on the other side. She nodded, knowing I had assigned her the long route because she was quieter and faster than I was. Tonight would be these soldiers' last. I took no pleasure in that.

As she slipped along the ground toward the structure, a familiar voice rang out from the darkness, surprising us. We froze in our tracks.

"Well, well, Aaron of Rivershire. I worried you'd be smarter than this."

Dumont stepping into the light from behind the stable to which Edweene was headed made my blood run cold. He drew his sword, and a cruel smile played across his lips. In my mind, I still held him as a friend—perhaps we'd arrived here, together by The God's providence. Edweene was not so naïve; she drew her sword and let any pretense of stealth pass from her body. She coiled, ready to strike.

"Dumont?" My voice was barely a whisper, "What are you doing? Your brother is within—"

I cut my comment short as six Golish warriors stepped from the darkness behind him, flanking him, their weapons ready. My heart sank with dread and disbelief.

Betrayer is all I could think of—an Honorless Betrayer. "What is the meaning of this?" I asked, my voice still a whisper.

I squared up with my knife, and the lych did likewise. She was closer, if it came to killing, she'd take him first.

Dumont's smile widened, a mocking glint in his eyes. "Oh, Aaron. So naive, so trusting. Did you really think I would follow you on this foolish quest? That I would risk everything for the sake of one man?"

Edweene's eyes narrowed, her hand tightening on the hilt of her sword. "You treacherous bastard," she hissed. "You've betrayed us. I knew you would."

Dumont laughed, the sound harsh and grating. "Betrayed? No, my dear abomination. I've simply seen the truth. The Crusade needs this war,

Aaron. It needs the fire, fury, and righteous anger that only battle can bring to hold it together. And I will not let you or anyone else stand in the way."

My mind reeled, and I struggled to reconcile the man I had known with the traitor who stood before me. "Dumont, please," I pleaded. Unfortunately, desperation crept into my voice for a singular moment. "Think about what you're doing. This isn't you. This isn't the man I know."

But Dumont's face hardened, all traces of humor vanishing. "You never knew me, Aaron. None of you did. You were all too blinded by your own self-righteousness, your own narrow view of the world. But I see clearly now. I see what must be done."

He turned to the Golish warriors, his voice ringing with authority. "Take them."

The warriors surged forward, their weapons flashing in the dim light.

Edweene moved first, but they were already at a charge, and they passed by Dumont before she could reach him, so she cut down the lead Gol. He fell, dead and grasping at his throat. She sashayed sideways and deflected the downswing of the second. Three more rushed past her toward me. In a flash, I drew my dagger with my off hand and put it in the face of the lead warrior, and he too dropped, not dead, but screaming in pain and clawing at the blade embedded in his flesh.

I lost sight of Edweene as the other two were on me. Their sword skills were admirable but they trained for formation. And this combat was open. I dashed to the side, putting the one out of the battle, blocked by the boxes and gear beside the tent. The other came in fast, shield high, and sword held ahead. I knocked it quickly aside and shoulder-smashed into his shield, surprising him and sending him back a step. He found his footing and came back, but it was too late. I was inside his shield, and I drove my knife into his armpit and through the gambeson there. He gasped; his eyes told me he was dying. He fell back, clutching at his side and gulping air. He dropped to the ground on his knees. My knife went with him.

I snatched his dropped sword up and turned on his companion just as a crossbow bolt grazed across my thigh and thudded into the boxes. I turned for a split second to look and saw another squad of Gols approaching, led by a large, experienced-looking Tartan sergeant with a rank of crossbow troops at their front. From the corner of my eye, I also saw the two at the front of the tent coming around the corner, accompanied by even more.

"Stop this madness, Aaron. You are done," Dumont spoke loudly. "And hold your arrows, men." He held out his hands, and the rank of crossbowmen stayed their hands.

There were too many, and soon we found ourselves surrounded, our backs pressed against the wall of crates and boxes along the tent. Edweene, a little ahead of me, pulled her blade from a fallen man's guts. All three of her opponents were dead, scattered around her in a rough semi-circle. She stood, faced them, and backed her way next to me. Sweat poured down my face as I struggled to catch my breath.

"You fell into our ruse, man," Dumont sneered, his face twisting with contempt. "You and your hellish abomination. Yes, I know what she is. And it was simple. You are predictable."

My heart pounded in my chest. My breath came in ragged gasps. I looked left. Then right. "I will kill you, betrayer," I snarled, my voice low and dangerous.

"No. Aaron. I will," said Edweene. "And consume you . . ." She added.

Dumont hesitated a moment, a grim look of hate and disgust spreading across his face. Then he composed himself and laughed again, the sound grating and mirthless. "You shall try. But I have bested you here. Now, these men shall kill you. And I shall make sure that this war begins. And the Gols have their land back, and here I will be a prince among princes."

As the Golish warriors closed in, their blades glinting with deadly promise, my mind raced, desperately searching for a way out. But there was none. The Golish warriors closed in, their blades glinting with deadly promise, leaving us trapped, outnumbered, and outmatched with no hope of escape.

Edweene laughed. "We've been here before, Aaron. We have not seen our last day."

How can she be so confident? I readied the Golish sword, gripping it until it settled comfortably in my hand. "Come then, you coward Dumont. Edweene was right about you all along. I'll kill you today first," I said, looking at the big sergeant. "And then, you . . ."

"You dare—" Dumont started forward as he spoke.

But before he could finish, the sergeant interrupted him. "My lord, the Tawl demanded we bring them." Dumont looked aghast, angry, ready to burst. His eyes narrowed at the sergeant, and his body tensed.

And just like that, Edweene was right. The God worked through the abomination even, I realized. At least for a moment, we were spared.

"Drop your weapons," he said. "You are not to be killed now."

Realizing our providence, I said, "Very well," and gave Dumont a glare that mocked his lack of power here. "And you thought you'd be a prince among princes. Already you see your power here," I said. Edweene and I dropped our weapons and raised our arms to our sides to show we had no blades in our sleeves.

The Tartan sergeant gave us a quick, cursory look, then four of their warriors seized us, their rough hands gripping our arms and twisting them behind our backs. They dragged us towards the tent where Ser Prenot was being held.

We did not struggle. There would be no use. Another twenty had formed a semi-circle around us. Waiting was our game now. This seemed so familiar. Edweene and I seemed to have a knack for such things.

When we entered, it took a moment for my eyes to adapt to the dim light. The space was expansive, with a central pole that reached upwards to support the heavy canvas roof. Once-ornate carpets, now stained and soaked with the blood of countless victims, covered the ground, obscuring their intricate patterns with dark, rusty hues. Boxes and crates filled with various supplies and sinister-looking implements cluttered one side of the tent in a haphazard manner. In the center of the space stood a large, wooden table, its surface covered in a grisly array of tor-ture devices, from razor-sharp blades and hooks to cruel-looking clamps and brands, all stained with the blood and viscera of those unfortunate enough to find themselves at the Tawl's mercy. The air was thick with the coppery scent of blood and the stench of decay, a testament to the hor-rors that had taken place within these canvas walls.

Kneeling on the ground was young Ser Prenot. The young knight kneeled on the ground, his face bruised and bloodied, his eyes hollow with pain and exhaustion. But the sight of the figures standing over him in this grisly place made my heart stop in my chest.

The Tawl, his dark armor seeming to absorb the light, stood with his arms crossed. A cruel smile played across his lips. He was as dark and fright-ening as he was at Lord Duveaux's estate. The power of the Old Gods radiated off the man in waves of despair. I breathed deeply and readied myself for what was to come. His helmet was on a table beside him, and his cloak was thrown over a peg in the tent's central pole. Dumont moved in beside him and looked down at his brother with a sneer of contempt.

"Dumont?" Ser Prenot's voice was a ragged whisper, disbelief and confusion etched across his battered face. "What . . . what are you doing here? Why are you with the Gols?"

But Dumont ignored him, his gaze fixed on me with smug satisfaction. "I told you, Aaron," he said, his voice dripping with disdain. "You were predictable. And now, you've played right into our hands."

The Tawl chuckled, the sound like the scrape of a blade across a bone. "You thought you could free this weasel," he said, his eyes glinting with malice. "Ser Dumont here told us you held a fool's honor. That you would come to free him, he said you were a fool for lost causes and rescues," he shot a look at Edweene. "It seems he was right.

"Why did you lure us here?" I said, finally understanding that this was never about the Crusade for the Tawl. There was something more basic in the reasoning, something darker.

"That answer is simpler than you may think," he said, stepping forward and running a finger along Edweene's cheek. "Yes. It is much simpler."

"Leave her be," I snapped. "And tell me."

"Does she wear her ring," Aaron of Rivershire. Or do you?".

Behind the Tawl, Dumont shifted. He was uncomfortable and nervous. I noticed he held my long knife in his hand. He must have retrieved it from the dead man outside. My family's honor in a traitor's hand filled my heart with rage. But the Tawl was the pressing matter right now.

"I don't know what you are talking about."

"You don't?" he asked. You killed my sorcerer, boy. And stole his toy. I wanted it back. And . . . what kind of dreadful warrior would I be if I let someone slip into my camp, kill my general and my sorcerer, and not find a little revenge?"

"We will win this war and take our land back for the Old Gods."

"It is our land; it was always ours before you took it. The—"

"Perspective," he said, cutting me off. He gestured to Dumont, who stood tall and proud, his hand resting on the hilt of his sword. "Your friend here has seen the truth. He knows that the Gols will triumph, that the Old Gods are the only true path to power and glory."

I shook my head, my mind reeling with the enormity of their betrayal. "You're insane," I said, my voice trembling with rage. "Both of you. This war will bring nothing but death and suffering. Can you not see that?"

But Dumont only laughed, the sound harsh and grating. "Death and suffering are the price of victory," he said, eyes blazing with a fanatic zeal I had never seen before. "The Old Gods demand it, and we shall deliver it unto them."

Beside me, Edweene tensed, her hands curling into fists. I could feel the power emanating from her, the dark energy that coursed through her undead veins. But even she could not hope to prevail against the Tawl and Dumont, not here, not now.

"And now," the Tawl said, his voice a low, menacing growl, "you two will die together. A fitting end for those who would defy the will of the Old Gods," he motioned toward me and Prenot.

Then he pointed at Edweene, "And this is where
you are returned to your rightful owner."

CHAPTER 13
THE TAWL

"D umont?" Ser Prenot's voice was a ragged whisper. The man's battered face showed disbelief and confusion etched across it. "What . . . what is going on here? Why are you with these heathen Gols?"

Dumont ignored him, his gaze fixed on me. His face was all smug satisfaction. "I told you, Aaron," he said, his voice dripping with disdain. "You were predictable. I don't understand all this talk about Edweene and don't care, but we will have our war, and that is what matters."

The Tawl chuckled, the sound like the scrape of a blade across a bone. "You thought you could save this wretched creature," he said, his eyes glinting with malice as he gestured to Edweene.

"But she belongs to me, as she once belonged to my sorcerer."

I felt Edweene tense beside me, her hands curling into fists. "I belong to no one," she hissed, her voice dangerous.

The Tawl's smile widened. "Ah, but you do, my dear. That ring on your finger, the one you guard so jealously... it is your phylactery, is it not? The vessel that holds your very soul?"

My mind reeled as the pieces fell into place. I thought back to when Edweene had been a slave to the necromancer Kau Fah. She had told me the power the ring held. I'd witnessed him torture her with it. It wasn't simply some appendage that could control her with sorcery. It was her soul in that ring. Without it, she was but an emotionless, helpless, person-less shell. Edweene's ring, the source of her power and the key to her existence ... This is what the Tawl wanted. We were lured here because of this. He wanted his slave-assassin back. If the Tawl got it, he could enslave her, bend her to his will like a puppet on a string. Like the necromancer, we killed to free her.

"You will never have it," Edweene said, her eyes blazing with defiance. "I would rather die than be a slave again. We killed your necromancer, Kau Fah, and perhaps we'll do the same for you, savage."

Dumont scoffed, his face twisting with disgust. "You are an abomination," he spat. "A creature of darkness and evil. You deserve nothing but death. Slavery is a mercy."

I whirled on him, my anger rising and my heart racing. I glared hard at him and locked eyes with the man I had seen as my companion. There was no respect there anymore, only contempt and rage. "I'll kill you first, traitor," I said.

Dumont's eyes narrowed, and his grip tightened on my weapons. "You are a fool, Aaron. Sentiment blinds you and misplaced loyalty. The Crusade is a farce. You, of all people, believe this. And the Gols are in the greater position. The war must continue, and we must have the land."

I knew much of what he said was right, though I was loath to admit it or even ponder too long upon it. The Crusade had been losing ground for years, and the Gols' superior numbers and ruthless tactics had pushed us back at every turn. We still held the Holy Land, but for how long if the Crusade began campaigning? If Dumont truly believed that siding with the enemy was the only way to survive, perhaps he knew something the rest of us did not. I would see his gambit fail.

The Tawl's laughter filled the tent, cold and mocking. "You see, Ser Aaron? Your friend here understands the truth. The Old Gods demand blood and suffering, and we shall give it to them."

He turned to Edweene, his hand outstretched. "Give me the ring, and I will spare your companion. Refuse, and I will make you watch as I flay the flesh from their bones."

Edweene's eyes met mine, a silent communication passing between us. I saw the resolve in her gaze, the determination to protect me and Ser Prenot at any cost. But I also saw the fear, the knowledge of what awaited her if she surrendered her ring.

My thoughts flashed to my sister back home in Rivershire. I wondered if she knew of my plight, and if she could sense the danger I faced. The memory of her tearful farewell before I set out on this cursed mission haunted me. Had I made the right choice, leaving her behind to pursue vengeance and redemption in the Holy Land? Would I ever see her again, or would my quest end here, so far from home? The thought of never returning, of leaving my sister alone in the world, filled me with a profound sense of guilt and longing just then . . . I'd come here for something important, I told myself, and I left everything else behind. And then, I saw my sister in Edweene's blue eyes, locked in someone's mind, beholden to their every command, and I wondered how Edweene had endured so much and how she'd survived. She was so strong, and I could not abide such things. This hateful thing was so much more than just the pain Edweene endured. Edweene's plight was just its manifestation in one soul.

"No," I said, my voice ringing out in the tent. "We will not give in to your demands, Tawl. We will fight and prevail, as we always have."

The Tawl's face contorted with rage, his hand reaching for Edweene's wrist. But before he could reach her, Dumont moved faster than I would have thought possible. In a blur of steel, he drove my long knife into the Tawl's back; the blade sank deep into the flesh until the point exited the bastard's chest, spraying droplets of red blood over Edweene.

The Tawl staggered forward against Edweene, his eyes wide with shock and pain. He turned, his mouth opening in a silent scream, and then he fell, full onto her, taking her to the ground with a dull thud.

For a moment, there was silence, broken only by the ragged sound of our breathing. Then, chaos erupted. I looked down at the Tawl's lifeless body, the hilt of my own knife protruding from his back. Dumont's betrayal had been sudden and shocking, but there was no time to dwell on it now. We had to act, or we'd be in the dirt with him.

Stunned by the sudden events, the Golish took a moment to figure out what was happening. In that crucial moment, Edweene shoved the body off her and rose to meet them, pulling the Tawl's scimitar from his scabbard as though she'd rehearsed it. Bolts of dark energy crackled from her fingertips and up along the blade as she stepped into her fighting stance.

I leaped forward and shouldered into Dumont, sending him sprawling to the floor. I spun and grabbed an iron-bound torch from a nearby sconce, hammering it into Dumont's face as he struggled to get to his feet, sending him into a daze. I turned to face the remaining warriors. Beside me, Ser Prenot struggled to his feet but was unwell and his hands tied.

"Why, Dumont?" he rasped, his voice was thick with pain and disbelief. "Why would you betray us, betray your own brother? How could you turn your back on . . . on everything?" He fell back to his knees, lost in his brother's disgrace and his own personal demons. To see your delusions crushed in such a manner is not an easy thing to face. I'd seen it outside Clurak when I had slain Edweene the first time, cursing her to this half-life. I'd seen it when I'd discovered the bishop turned coat. It would take a moment—a moment we didn't have, but one I'd do my best to give him.

I looked at the big sergeant and said, "Remember when I said I'd kill you first? Now's the time, heathen. You should have killed me when the traitor ordered it."

"It is not a worry, Crusader. I'll have you, and then I'll have the traitor and his brother," he growled back.

The four Gol warriors lunged forward, led by the big sergeant, their weapons drawn—all spears, except the sergeant who wielded his giant curved scimitar. He came in hard toward me. I swung low at his legs, as I ducked beneath a mighty swing. It took him wide, but my makeshift club deflected from his armored sabatons. He corrected and deftly changed his weapon's direction to bring it down on me. I was out of position and raised the torch above me to deflect the swing. But it never reached me as Edweene's crackling blade slid through his steel plate like paper. He cried and fell back as she pushed more dark energy into the blade. He convulsed on the weapon, then slid to the ground, seemingly dead and smoking.

"Forgot about me," she said. "Now that was a mistake."

The other four Gol's stepped back as their leader sizzled and burned before them. But then the flap flew open, and several more could be seen gathering outside—likely the whole bunch we'd left there. There was no way we could get out that way without being slaughtered, even if we were able to dispatch the four in front of us.

One of the four called out to his friends, "They have murdered the Tawl, they are escaping! Sound the alarm!"

Another cried, "They have a wytch!"

To my left, Edweene fell against me and groaned.

"Took a lot out of me," she hasped. "There must be a way out. I'm spent. We must be gone."

There was nowhere to go.

CHAPTER 14
ESCAPE INTO DARKNESS

The tent was about to become a death trap for us. Our apprehension hung heavy in the air. The four stared at us, each daring the other with their actions to be the first to rush us but afraid of what the lych might do to them. Their leader still lay, his corpse blackening, smoking husk, between us. None of them wanted that. None of them wanted the lych's curse.

But it would not be long before one of them worked up the courage, and it would be like releasing a storm, a dam breaking. The four remaining Gols, along with all their allies outside, would pour into the tent then, and they would finish us.

"Looks as if we're trapped," I said. As I did so, I reached over and pulled my knife from The Tawl's back and snatched his dagger from his belt, tucking it into mine. I'd not leave my weapon here to serve Ser Dumont's purpose. I then sliced the ropes, binding Ser Prenot.

"Thank you," he said and rubbed his wrists together.

Opposite, one of the Gols got a little courageous and eased himself forward.

Edweene gasped and leaned harder against me. She slipped her hand in my offhand. "We'll perish together as comrades," she whispered. "Knight of the Crusade and Abomination against The God." She laughed a bit, then breathed deeply. I could feel her pain in her lightening grip.

"As more than comrades," I sighed and repeated quietly. ". . . more than comrades."

She squeezed my hand. "I have little strength left, Aaron. If we are going to act, let's do it now so that I may take some of them with me before they have me." She knew she'd not die while the ring was still intact, but that didn't mean she'd be able to move. Exhaustion and debilitation were still very much a thing for her. Then they'd take her and the ring, and they'd have their lych.

I squeezed her hand in response—a tiny symbol of my commitment to her—and whispered a prayer to The God for salvation. "I suppose there is no way out, Ser Prenot," I joked. "Perhaps there is some secret tunnel beneath this torture tent?"

Ser Prenot gasped, his face pale beneath the grime and blood. Even as the words left my lips, a flicker of memory passed across his face. He turned to me, his eyes wide with sudden realization.

"The tunnel," he said, his voice low and urgent. He coughed and bent over at the waist. "Yes . . . the Tawl had a secret way out of the camp, a tunnel dug beneath this tent so he could question me in private—or cut on me, as he would. You, Ser, are brilliant."

My heart leaped for a moment. God provides, as always. But my joy and faith were tempered by the knowledge that the warriors were still standing between us and our escape. Never is a prayer answered without a trial for worthiness. We had to act fast before they found their courage and surged toward us—and our chance was lost forever.

"Where? Where is this tunnel, man?"

"There, he said, beyond the table with the tools." He pointed eight or ten paces away, behind the blood-infused table holding the pokers, clamps, and knives, "Beneath that bench and tarpaulin."

"Edweene," I said, my voice tight. "Do you have the strength to provide us some time?"

The lych nodded, her face pinched, eyes narrowed and hard. She closed her eyes and focused—a silent incantation and channeling of some dark sorcery. For a moment, nothing happened. Then, the air in the tent began to shimmer, coalesce into an ethereal darkness that warped into something discernable—and altogether frightening. A figure took shape in the center of the room.

It was a thing of nightmares, pulled from the pages of The Book of Arian, and the Six Tenants of The God, a twisted phantasm of shadow and smoke, its form vaguely human but stretched and distorted in ways that made the mind reel. The Golish warriors cried out in terror, stumbling back from the apparition, their weapons falling from their nerveless fingers. The phantasm advanced, its movements jerky and unnatural, its eyes burning with an unholy light. The warriors turned and fled, pushing through the heretofore open tent flaps, their screams echoing in the night as they burst from the tent and disappeared into the darkness beyond. The crowd of Gols outside likewise stepped back and away, letting the flap fall closed.

The phantasm dissipated as soon as they left, fading into a cloud of smoke that curled and eddied around the tent before disappearing entirely. Edweene sagged against me, her face ashen with exhaustion.

"Hurry," she whispered, her voice weak and thready. "I don't have much strength left."

Ser Prenot was already moving, his pain-filled limping and shuffling slowly. With all these wounded allies, I wondered if we had any chance at all. With what little strength he had, he shoved aside the old table and crates that lined the tent's back wall. Behind them, he flipped open a makeshift pit-covering and a dark hole gaped in the earth. Edweene and I hobbled over and looked down, me holding Edweene upright with my hand around her waist.

The rough-hewn walls of a tunnel descended into shadow, and a rickety wooden ladder led downward into the darkness. It wasn't deep, I could see the bottom with the light of the torch I'd grabbed.

"This way," he said, gesturing for us to follow.

We descended into the tunnel. The wooden ladder creaked as we descended. First, Prenot, followed by Edweene, who struggled and gasped as she went. I watched the tent opening as they descended, my heart pounding out my impatience as I turned my knife over and over in my hand—a nervous twitch when my anxiety peaked. And finally, they called up to me, and I went down, pulling the little door shut as I did.

The air was damp and musty, and the darkness pressed around us like a physical thing.

We moved as quickly as we could, our breath coming in ragged gasps, our hearts pounding in our chests. After what felt like an eternity, but it could have been no longer than a few minutes, we reached the end of the tunnel. Ser Prenot pushed open a hidden trapdoor and went up. After emerging, he called us and we ascended.

Edweene and I pulled ourselves from the tunnel, gasping for air and blinking in the sudden brightness of the stars, I felt a wave of exhaustion wash over me. My body ached with the weight of the morning's harrowing activities, and my mind reeled with the shock of Dumont's betrayal. Beside me, Edweene swayed, her face pale and drawn. I reached to steady her, my hand finding hers in the darkness. We simply crouched there for a moment, taking in the magnitude of what we had just survived; I focused completely on holding her steady.

"We've almost made it," I whispered, my voice hoarse and raw but trying to give her hope. "By the grace of The God, almost."

Edweene nodded, her eyes glinting with a fierce determination. "Not yet Aaron. Not yet."

She waved her hand outward. "We're not free yet. Concentrate on that, Aaron. Not on me, or we'll all perish. Do what you must to get us out. I'll not be enslaved again."

With a shock, I realized that we were still within the Golish camp, albeit obscured behind a short wall and hanging curtains of sailcloth one might find in a make-shift testament booth. The curtain was open, and the tents and cookfires stretched out around us in a sea of flickering shadows. In the distance, the sun was rising over the horizon, and the black sky was giving away to gray and bloody orange. We could hear the sounds of alarm, the shouts of warriors, and the clash of steel as they rushed toward our old hiding place. Many of them carried torches and buckets of pitch. I realized they intended to burn us to death in Prenot's torture tent.

"We need to move," I said, my voice low and urgent. "Stay in the shadows and avoid any contact if you can."

We set out across the camp. There was no chance to be silent in our current state—Edweene and Prenot struggling and wounded as they were—so we were smart, slipping between tents and in the darkened shadows thrown out by the watchfires. We kept our our cloaks around our heads, and our weapons ready. The chaos caused by the Tawl's death and the phantasm's appearance worked in our favor better than we'd hoped. The Golish warriors were in a panic, and too distracted to notice three fleeing shadows.

Still, there were close calls. More than once, we had to flatten ourselves against the ground or duck behind cover as a group of Gol soldiers passed by, their eyes scanning the darkness for any sign of trouble. Each time, I held my breath, certain that we would be discovered, that our escape would be cut short in a hail of arrows and steel. The whole time, except when it was held, my breath came short and hard, my heart pounding out my fear in rapid staccato. But, somehow, miraculously, we made it through. We reached the edge of the camp, the dark line of the Devil's Forest looming before us like a promise of safety. Edweene leaned heavily against me, her breath coming in ragged gasps, her face pale with pain and exhaustion.

"Almost there," I murmured, my arm tightening around her waist. "Just a little further."

As we made our way to the edge of the Devil's Forest, my mind wandered to the past few days' events. Dumont's betrayal, the revelation of the Tawl's dark designs, and this miserable escape seemed like a nightmare, a fever dream.

Beside me, Ser Prenot stumbled, his wounds and exhaustion taking their toll. I reached out to steady him with my other hand. My heart ached for the pain he must be feeling. To have one's own brother turn against them, to see the depths of his madness and cruelty he was taken by. To see him struck down in front of him—it was a burden no one should have to bear.

"I'm sorry," I murmured, my voice low and rough. "For everything you've endured, for the choices your brother made. You deserved better than this."

Ser Prenot shook his head, his eyes haunted and hollow. "I keep asking myself how I could have been so blind, how I could have missed the signs of his corruption. But in the end, it wasn't my fault, was it? The Crusade, the Church—it's all rotten to the core, poisoned by greed and fanaticism and the lust for power."

"Not all," I said.

And Edweene scoffed at that. "Ever the idealist, Aaron."

I tried my best to ignore her—and my own doubts and fears, which I kept buried deep. "We've all been complicit in this, Ser. We've all played our part in it. But that doesn't mean we can't strive for something better. The Six Tenets are real. We can believe in those."

Ser Prenot looked at me, his gaze searching and intense. "Do you really believe that?"

I hesitated; the weight of my own sins was heavy enough for ten men. But in the end, I knew there was only one answer I could give. "We have to believe it, Ser Prenot. We must believe in the Tenets . . . and redemption. Otherwise, what is the point of any of this?"

Ser Prenot nodded, his shoulders straightened, and we pressed on into the dark woods. We were three broken people seeking redemption and fleeing certain death.

As our trek lapsed into quiet, an explosion erupted behind us, throwing the early morning grayness into a flash of yellow and orange. Some flammable weapon had set the tent alight, blowing it to pieces. A wave of heat rushed through the camp, propelling us along. *Thank God we'd escaped that inferno*, I thought. With providence, they'd think we had been consumed in the conflagration.

But even as the words took form in my mind, a figure emerged from the shadows before us, blocking our path. It was Dumont, his sword drawn and his face a mask of rage, bloodied and burned. Blood poured from the wound where I'd brained him.

"You didn't think it would be that easy, did you?" he snarled, his eyes glinting with a feverish light. "I knew you would come this way. It's the only path that makes sense."

"How did you get here—"

"Before you?" he laughed aloud. But it was lost in the chaos behind us. "I watched you go down the hole. And I followed you in. The difference was—I didn't have to hide behind all the damn tents and avoid the Gols."

My heart was still thumping hard, and my breath was labored. I struggled to get it under control. We'd come too far to be thwarted now. I pulled Edweene in and held her close. Dumont's face twisted in disgust.

"Prenot," I said. I tried to keep the trepidation from my voice.

"Yes . . ." he responded.

"Take Edweene and go. I'm going to kill your brother."

"Yes, stupid brother, take the abomination away. I'll be sure to catch you and kill you both later."

"Dumont, I . . ."

"Prenot," I cut him off. "Ignore the traitorous basterd," he is no longer your brother. He no longer walks with The God. He has betrayed the Crusade, The Archbishop and violated every precept of the Book of Arian.

The knight hesitated, his eyes flickering between me and his brother. But he knew, as well as I did, that we had no choice. He nodded, his jaw trembling. A brave man, he'd resisted the tortures of the Tawl. Now, he was being asked to flee into the night with an enemy of the Temple while another fought his battle—against his own kin, no less. He tentatively took Edweene's arm.

She latched on to him and looked at me pleadingly. She wished to stay. She always thought she could handle more than she could. I shook my head as Dumont laughed.

"Go," I said to them.

Half-carrying her, they staggered off towards the tree line.

I turned back to Dumont, my long knife raised and ready. "It doesn't have to be this way," I pleaded. "We can still end this madness, find another path. I am sure your Breaking on the Star would only last a few moments."

But Dumont only laughed, the sound harsh and mocking in the night air. "You still don't understand, do you, Aaron? There is no other path. The Crusade must continue, no matter the cost. It is the Will of The God. And the Breaking would be yours when I tell the bishop how you interfered with his plan. For it was not mine."

And with that, he lunged forward, his blade flashing in a deadly arc.

I met his attack with a parry of my own: his sword and my long knife clashing in a shower of sparks. He pushed harder against my arm, driving me back, before pulling away, feinting low left, and rotating the attack higher and down. I caught his feint and deflected it away, bringing my blade down to slide across his armored chest. I stepped away, as did he to gain distance. I drew the Tawl's dagger with my offhand.

Two-weaponed now, I faced his larger sword, which he grasped with two hands. We circled each other slowly, like two dangerous predators looking for an opening in the other's defense. He was strong, and fast, skilled with his weapon as I was with mine. But his eye was swollen shut, and he kept adjusting his stance to account for his blindness. Every few seconds, he'd wipe the blood from his eye with his tunic by lowering his head and raising his shoulder to it. Never did he take his eye off me, but he was hurt. And that was my opening, I surmised.

He must have known what I was thinking. He smiled at me after he wiped his eye. "Yes, Aaron, you took your strike and nearly killed me—and a dishonorable attack it was. But this wound won't stop me from killing you. Take your shot, Hero of the Crusade, and find my sword in your gullet."

"You speak to me of dishonor—" I started, then in an attempt to throw him off, I lunged in with my knife, hoped to lure his parry. But he was too skilled. He saw it coming, and simply stepped back instead, keeping his guard in perfect position.

"You'll have to do better than tha—"

I didn't wait for him to finish, and drove in with my knife, seeing a tree behind him, and knowing he could not retreat. He deflected the dagger but left his side open. I slashed down with my long knife, which again, deflected from his mail forearm, but cut a shallow ribbon across his upper hand, barely penetrating the leather under his gauntlet.

And he was on me, coming in hard between my knives. He shouldered into me, knocking me back and off balance, then drove his sword down at my throat in a short, overhand slash. I rotated partially out of the way and parried it with my dagger. But the sword slid off the smaller blade, and struck my arm, cutting through my leather and slicing across my upper arm. I barely held my knife and retreated.

He grinned. "Now we're even, Hero."

"Hardly," I said. But he was right. Blood was flowing from my arm, soaking my tunic and gloves and slicking my grip. I wasn't sure how long I could last with such a wound. We danced back and forth, our blades moving in a blur of feints, parries, and attacks. Dumont was skilled, his movements precise and calculated But I was, as well. It was an equal match. But, I was losing strength. And he was also tired, his wounds slowing him down. I could hear his breath in ragged gasps even over my thundering heart and my own desperate breathing. Worse, I could feel my mind slacking, the loss of blood taking its toll on me.

I had to end this now, one way or another.

"Why, Dumont?" I panted, my voice condescending and accusatory. I tried to goad him.

"Why betray everything we fought for? Why turn your back on your own brother? You know this is not the God's Will. The bishop thumbs his nose at the Archbishop, who has declared this Crusade defensive."

Dumont's face twisted with a bitter smile; his eyes gleamed with a zealot's fire. "You speak of betrayal, but it is you who have betrayed The God, Aaron. The Archbishop has become weak, responding to complaints from the Northern Kingdoms. It is The God that declares Crusades. It is not to be managed by petty kings on petty thrones far away. You and your abomination, your lych lover. The Crusade, the Holy Land, is the only thing that matters, the only thing that can save us. We must drive these degenerate heathens from the darkness that threatens to engulf us all."

I shook my head, my heart heavy with the weight of his words. "You're wrong," I said, my voice low and fierce. I understood the desire to end this war, and an offensive war seemed the only way sometimes. But it was not this time. We had all suffered too much. "The darkness is within us, Dumont. It's in the hatred and fear that we cling to, the blind obedience to your need for war has lost its way. The Gol are strong. Too strong now."

Dumont's eyes narrowed, and his jaw clenched with rage. He lunged forward, his blade seeking my heart. But I was ready for him. I sidestepped the blow, brought my own knife up, and drove into a wicked jab. The blade bit deep into the flesh where his breastplate met the pauldron of his sword arm.

Dumont cried out in pain, his sword clattering to the ground. He staggered back, clutching at the wound, his face twisted with agony—and hatred.

Sparing not a moment of time, I advanced quickly on him, the instincts of an assassin driving me on. My conscience told me to call to him and decry. *It's over, Dumont, yield, and I will spare your life.* But I remembered his threats to Edweene and his curses against The God's Archbishop, and suddenly, there was no quarter in me. I pressed him against the tree and slipped my dagger up under his breastplate and into his abdomen. I saw the air escape his lungs, pinkish bubbling blood oozing between the steel and flesh, hot, dying breath on my face. I watched the soul start to leave his body in his dark, hard eyes . . . and something inside me cursed my nature and my need for vengeance and my depraved love of war . . .

But even as the soul fled his yes, I heard a cry from the edge of the forest. I turned, my heart in my throat, and saw Edweene stumble, her legs giving out beneath her. Ser Prenot caught her, his face a mask of anguish and desperation. I hesitated, torn between my desire for vengeance and my duty to my companions. But in the end, there was no choice. I turned and ran, leaving Dumont bleeding and broken behind me.

I reached Edweene's side just as she collapsed, her eyes fluttering closed, her breath shallow and uneven. I gathered her in my arms, my heart pounding with fear and desperation.

"Edweene," I whispered, my voice cracking with emotion. "Stay with me. Please, stay with me."

But she did not answer, her body limp and unresponsive in my arms.

I looked up at Ser Prenot, my eyes wide with panic. "We have to get her to safety," I said, my voice urgent and strained. "She needs help, more than I can give her here."

I looked at Dumont there on the tree, life quickly fleeing him. I looked up at Prenot who stared at his dying brother. I looked at Edweene, who was struggling to stay conscience.

"Go. There's nothing to do for him. I'll stash her and catch up."

The knight nodded at me, his face grim with understanding. He plunged into the dark embrace of the Devil's Forest. I listened until he was well away, and I dragged Edweene's nearly lifeless body to Dumont, who stared at us with his final glare.

I pulled her hand up and pressed her palm against the dying knight's face. His eyes widened in horror. "Feed, Edweene, while you still can," I said. "Heal yourself."

And she did.

CHAPTER 15
A GATHERING STORM

Two days later, were walked as best we could through the gates of Caer Gorak. Edweene was fully healed—a fact I had explained to Prenot as some benefit of her majyk, not that she'd drained his brother of his life's essence. He seemed to have accepted that, and I felt guilty for the lie—but not guilty enough to tell him true—some things he did not need to know. I was exhausted and weary. My arm was infected and swollen, and I favored one leg to the other, having carried much of Prenot's weight on the other for much of this Journey. As we made our way through the fortress, I couldn't help but reflect on the trials we had faced and the losses we had suffered. The weight of Dumont's betrayal hung heavy on my heart, and I found myself wondering if the price we had paid for victory was truly worth it.

Despite my guilt, I felt a wave of relief wash over me. The ancient fortress, with its towering walls and flickering torches, seemed like a beacon of hope after the darkness and chaos of the Golish camp and the twisted trails and thickets of the Devil's wood. Beside me, Prenot hobbled like an old man, not the young knight he was. His face was drawn, and his eyes haunted.

Geoffroi de Lyanha greeted us in the court-yard. His eyes widened as he took in our battered appearance. He fixed his eyes on me but flashed them over Edweene and Prenot for only a moment. He did not recognize them, but his eyes held a question—and one I'd answer soon enough.

"Ser Aaron," he said, his voice grave. "We had feared the worst when we heard of a fight, an explosion. Rampant Gol patrols and ambuscades have been triggered upon our troops, even within our territories. It is a relief to see you alive, though I fear the news you bring is grim."

I nodded, and my throat tightened with emotion. "We have much to discuss, Ser Geoffroi. The Tawl's dark designs, Dumont's betrayal—the very future of the Crusade hangs in the balance. I fear the war will start in earnest again."

Geoffroi's face darkened, and he gestured for us to follow him inside. As we walked, I caught glimpses of the soldiers' faces, some filled with curiosity, others with sympathy, others with dread. It was clear that word of our ordeal had spread, and the gravity of our mission was not lost on those who would likely pay the toll in blood for the results of our mission.

In the Knight Commander's war room once again, I could not help thinking how different things those few days past as we began our foray into the Devil's Forest. I'd been standing next to Dumont, listening to Geoffroi tell us of Gol ambushes and patrols, and a quieter, stealthy route might be the more realistic one. I remember how Dumont resisted our desire for secrecy, and how that made sense now. And now, his brother stood next to me, rescued as he was from the grips of the Gol—and his traitorous brother. I shook those memories away.

"Your mission was not sanctioned, my lord," he said. "I know this now. I sent a bird to Lord Gavreaux while you were out. He was careful in his response. But I read between the lines."

I was grateful he did not send the bird to the king in Clurak. Matters now might have been different. "That is correct," I said. There was no need to lie. "The Knight Commander was aware of our mission but would not endorse it." I felt Edweene stiffen next to me. Her vendetta against the order of knights was not forgotten; I could feel it—a tenseness radiating off of her whenever I mentioned them or Gavreaux himself. That vengeance would have to be a different day, however. Today was our victory day.

"What do you suppose the king might say? I am a man of the king, not the Knights of the Passage."

"Let me recount my tale, Ser," I said, believing that he had already decided not to inform the king.

He nodded to me, and we recounted our tale in full, sparing no detail of the horrors we had faced. Ser Geoffroi listened intently; his brow furrowed with concern.

After I finished, Prenot nodded his ascent and said, "Thus it was, my Lord."

"This is grave news indeed," Geoffroi said at last. "I hazard to say the King will not find fault when the facts are disclosed. But, with the Tawl's dark magic and the growing unrest among the Gols, I fear the frontier is ready to burn at any moment."

I watched Prenot as Geoffroi spoke, seeing the weight of consequences his capture had set motion, etched in the lines of his face. He had borne the brunt of Dumont's betrayal, and I could only imagine the pain and confusion he must be feeling. But was that price enough, or too much? It was his foolhardiness that had begun this madness.

"Ser Prenot spoke up then, his voice heavy with grief. "And what of my brother, Ser Geoffroi? What is to be done about his betrayal?"

The commander sighed, his eyes filled with sympathy. "Your brother's actions were a grievous crime against the Crown and the Church, Ser, and have jeopardized the Crusade and the security of the Holy Land. But you are not to blame for his choices. I hope the King will not see fit to punish your house. Your family has been loyal subjects for generations, certainly longer than I've been alive. The burden of leadership is heavy, but I know that you will bear it with honor and courage. I hope the archbishop feels likewise. I will put in a good word and do what I can."

As the meeting ended, Ser Geoffroi promised to inform the King and the Archbishop of our findings. He said, "Prepare yourself to leave. The King may well wish to see you. But take some time—enough to rest and heal, both in body and in spirit."

We agreed and retired to the small tower apartment that had been arranged for the three of us. Edweene, of course, made her sleeping arrangements elsewhere. I don't know where. But we'd see her about, or I would see the damned cat or raven. And, in the days that followed, I found myself haunted by the memories of our ordeal. I knew that Dumont's eyes would haunt me as others have. I woke in the night more than once, my heart pounding and skin slick with sweat. Memories of his eyes as his soul left its shell convicted me.

Edweene was a constant presence at my side. Her reassuring words, never filled with remorse or apology, were a balm to my troubled soul. And yet, even as I drew strength from her presence, I couldn't shake the feeling that something had shifted between us. The horrors we had witnessed, the darkness we had faced, had changed us both in ways that were still unclear.

One evening, as we sat upon the battlement, watching the sun sink below the horizon, the Golish frontier dark and foreboding beneath it, I turned to her, my voice soft with concern. "Edweene, what troubles you so? I can see the weight of it upon you, like a physical thing."

She was silent for a long moment, her eyes distant and ghostly blue. "The darkness inside me, Aaron. It is my nature," she said at last. "And it grows stronger every day, fed by the horrors we have seen and the lives we have taken. It is difficult to defeat it in a battle of wills. When I am alone, or in secret, I often think of . . . of feeding . . ." she lapsed into silence, considered her words for a moment, and I saw a shadow fall over her face. Then she completed her thought, "Let us just say, I fear that one day, it will consume me entirely, and I will lose myself forever." And I don't know whom I will destroy on the way.

It was a portentous thought and one that frightened me. Her darkness was a weight I'd willingly borne, heretical as it may be. The enemy of God always lurked there underneath. I wondered if it would be me one day that fed her dark hunger. *She would never*, I promised myself, but not confidently. I remembered how voraciously she'd consumed Dumont. It was almost overwhelming. I tentatively took her hand in mine, faking strength as well as I could manage. My heart was buzzing, and my mind was churning a thousand pictures repeatedly—none of them good. Ultimately, I lied to her, as I often do to myself: "You are stronger than the darkness in you, Edweene. There is a light inside you that can never be extinguished.

She smiled a sad, sweet smile that made my heart ache even more. "A fool's notion, Aaron. Beautiful, but foolish," she hissed, and that aura of dread came over her, and her blue eyes flashed.

I wanted to argue with her, to convince her she was wrong, but the words stuck in my throat. Deep down, I knew there was a truth to what she said, a reality I had avoided for far too long.

She grinned disconcertingly—not happily. "I fed on Dumont like he was a tavern stew. And you took me to him, knowing I would. It must make you realize we are the culmination of our nature. Nothing more. Nothing less."

I had nothing to add, no way to contradict. At that moment, my mind wandered to my family's home in Rivershire. Had my sister, Elayne, moved on without me? A part of me yearned to leave the intrigues and bloodshed of the Holy Land behind, to return to the simplicity of home. But the weight of my duty held me back. I had sworn an oath to uncover the bishop's treachery, to see justice done. Could I abandon that sacred vow, even for the love of my sister, or even for Edweene? Edweene seemed to know me better than I knew myself. I had already decided. Long ago.

I pulled away from her, knowing that it hurt her. I regretted it, silently hoping she'd pull me back. But she let me go, anyway.

She laughed darkly and stood, brushing off her thighs, almost symbolically. "As it is, so it always shall be," she said. "I will leave tomorrow. For where, I don't know. Perhaps I will return to visit vengeance upon Gavreaux and—"

I stood and interrupted her, but she put up her hand. "No more, Aaron. Let me finish. And Perhaps I won't seek vengeance. Perhaps you've taught me something after all."

I sat back down. "Going with you is not possible for me. I must go to Clurak. I would visit the king and deal with the bishop. It must be so."

"And so it must, Aaron. We part ways again. Perhaps we shall find each other on your next adventure . . ."

I nodded, my heart heavy, knowing much strife lay ahead. The road to Clurak would be long and fraught with peril, and the challenges awaited me there were still unknown. But I knew I had to see this through to bring justice to those who betrayed us and ensure our sacrifices were not meaningless.

And so I watched her go, a part of me yearning to call out to her, to beg her to stay. But I knew that this was a path she had to walk alone, a battle she had to fight on her own terms. All I could do was hope that someday, somehow, she would find her way back to the light.

And she was gone.